THE 65 LAKH HEIST

THE 65 LAKH HEIST

SURENDER MOHAN PATHAK

Translated from the Hindi by
Sudarshan Purohit

BLAFT
PUBLICATIONS
PRIVATE LIMITED
CHENNAI

First published 1977 by Guide Pocket Books

Blaft Publications Pvt. Ltd.
#27 Lingam Complex
Dhandeeswaram Main Road
Velachery
Chennai 600042
email: blaft@blaft.com
website: www.blaft.com

Printed at Sudarsan Graphics, Chennai

Translator's Note

"This sort of hero was something new, a sensation," Surender Mohan Pathak recalls. "A wanted criminal, someone who actually murdered people, but still someone you could sympathize with. No one had done it before."

By 1971, Pathak had already written forty-eight novels, most of them featuring his popular press reporter hero, Sunil. But he was feeling rather constrained; many of the new plotlines he was coming up with didn't fit the moral, upright character of Sunil.

So Pathak created a new hero, Vimal. In his debut novel *Maut Ka Khel* (Game of Death), Vimal escaped from jail after having been framed by his wife. Two months later, the same character appeared in a second book, *Daulat Aur Khoon* (Money and Murder).

Yet the Vimal series almost died before it got anywhere. The first two books flopped. Pathak's publisher at the time, Meerut-based Aarti Pocket Books, told him that if he wrote any more stories with the new character, they wouldn't publish them.

Three years later, another publisher, Shanu Paperbacks, contacted Pathak to ask him whether he'd like to write for them. Pathak had already finished the third in the Vimal series, *Ishtihaari Mujrim* (Wanted Criminal). This plot was based on a real-life robbery of a Union Bank van in Delhi.

But this book, too, failed to sell, and Pathak decided to give up on Vimal.

Around the same time, Surender Mohan Pathak was becoming more famous for something else—the translation of James Hadley Chase novels into Hindi. Pathak's natural style and way with words suited these books well, and they became so popular that Pathak was now being hailed as a major writer, even if as a translator.

Pathak used this clout to push another of his original works onto the publisher, Guide Pocket Books, threatening that he'd stop doing the translations unless they printed it. The threat, Pathak himself says, was an empty one, since in those days he earned much less from his own work than from the Chase translations. Translating a Chase book was easier work, too, since he could do it in three or four days while sitting at his day job in the telephone company.

But Guide agreed. The book, the fourth starring Vimal, was a story about an improbable bank robbery—a safecracker's last big job. It was titled *Painsath Lakh Ki Dakaiti* (The 65 Lakh Heist) and was first published in May 1977. The cover of the first edition of the book claimed it was a "Sunil Series" novel—a ploy to get more readers.

It was a hit—fast-paced, with believable characters and plot twists, and an ending that left readers wanting more. The success of the book made Surender Mohan Pathak one of the best-known writers in the history of Hindi pulp. The novel went on to be published by seven different companies, and has been reprinted at least fifteen times, selling more than 3,00,000 copies so far.

Today, there are thirty-eight novels in the Vimal series, which is widely considered by fans to be Pathak's best work. The series has inspired several imitations and rip-offs, none of which has approached the success of the original. Fans look forward eagerly to each instalment of the series. Vimal has come a long way since his first book: he got remarried, learned to master the art of disguise, took on the Mumbai and Punjabi mafia, and became a protector of the innocent—all while being a wanted criminal himself.

But it really started back in May 1977 with *Painsath Lakh ki Dakaiti*—the beginning of a whole new world of crime fiction.

Until recently, Indian language pulp fiction had hardly been discussed in the English media. After *The Blaft Anthology of Tamil Pulp Fiction* generated some press, I contacted the publishers to see if I could talk them into bringing out some Hindi pulp translations as well. Since I read English faster than Hindi, I was hoping someone else would do it for me to buy and read.

But the publishers asked me whether I could do it all: researching authors, going through books to find good candidates for translation, doing the translation itself. Wondering to myself whether I could do it, I agreed.

The usual resource for research—the net—was little use in this case. Hindi popular fiction is almost entirely below the radar. There is, however, an Orkut fan club for Surender Mohan Pathak, from whose members I learned which were his most popular titles. I spent several months devouring a series of pulp novels (and bringing my Hindi reading speed up a lot). Once I'd read *Painsath Lakh Ki Dakaiti*, it was easy to understand why the book has spawned an entire genre of anti-hero crime fiction. Later on, when we went to Delhi to meet Pathakji, he told us it was one of his personal favourites as well.

There's no way I could have completed this project without the support of my wife Payal, who let me spend all my evenings on the computer; her parents, who found the books

I was looking for; my parents, who always made sure I read some Hindi; Rohit, who searched through dozens of libraries and shops to find the original editions of *Painsath Lakh Ki Dakaiti* and more; my Buaji, who pointed me to the right authors to research; George, Rohinton, Dinker and Nitika, who read versions of the text and encouraged me to keep going; and, of course, Rakesh, Kaveri and Rashmi of Blaft, who thought it was a good idea. Oriana Leckert's numerous suggestions have improved the text immeasurably. Thanks also to Sharad Srivastava, who runs the Surender Mohan Pathak fan club on Orkut, for his initial pointers.

Sudarshan Purohit
January 2009

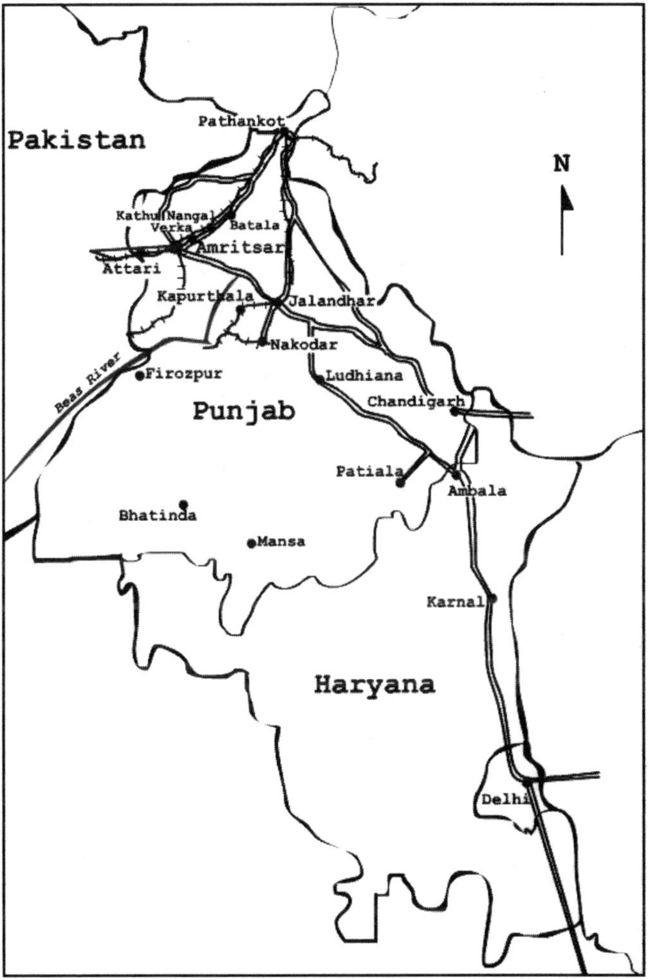

Pakistan
Pathankot
N
Kathu Nangal
Verka
Batala
Amritsar
Attari
Kapurthala
Jalandhar
Nakodar
Beas River
Firozpur
Ludhiana
Chandigarh
Punjab
Patiala
Ambala
Bhatinda
Mansa
Karnal
Haryana
Delhi

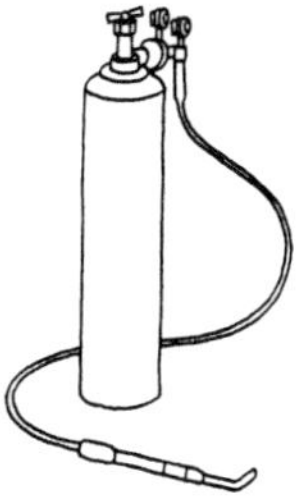

1

MAYARAM LIT A NEW CIGARETTE and looked at his watch.

It was time.

He'd found out beforehand what time Karnail Singh's shift at Mehta House ended. Now he was here, waiting.

Mehta House was a vast four-storey building on Lawrence Road, and it housed the bank and the vault around which Mayaram's plans revolved. Everyone said the vault was impregnable, but Mayaram planned to prove them all wrong. This would be the last big job of his life. And failure would mean a slow, lingering death in prison.

Mayaram Bawa was well known for just one thing: opening safes. His almost magical ability to crack any safe he got his hands on had led his accomplices and even the police to call him "Ustad". He'd been to jail five times so far—the last time, he'd had to breathe that stale prison air for seven years, the longest term he'd served. He'd been released three and a half years ago, his body worn out from the grind of hard labour. Now he was forty-five years old, and he knew that if he went in again, only his corpse would come out.

The thought sent shivers through his body.

Every minute of the last three and a half years, all he'd thought about was how to pull off one last big job, and then retire in peace. Now, at last, the wait was over. The police had finally lost interest in him; it was time to act on the plan that had been rattling around his brain since before he'd been released. The success or failure of this plan would determine the rest of his life.

This time there would be no mistake. No irresponsible, inexperienced louts on the team. Nothing would trip him up, send him to jail again. He'd planned each step very carefully. He would work under no one. He wouldn't let any other idiot's screw-up bring him down. He had worked out every little detail, and everything would go the way he wanted it.

It was Mayaram's bad luck that every time he'd been caught, it had been because of some stupid accomplice's bungling. Or else the planners would overlook something important, and the police would be on them before they even reached the loot. The last time, he'd planted the explosives around the vault perfectly, but the fools making the plan hadn't realized that the door was wired to an alarm. Before he knew it, he was in jail—for seven long years.

But this time, it would be different. He'd created a foolproof plan for the heist, and now he was looking for the right people to carry it out.

He saw Karnail Singh coming down the steps of the bank. The Sikh had the white beard of an old man, but was solidly built. He was still wearing his security guard uniform. He stopped for a few moments on the steps to talk to some friends; then, still laughing at something, he left them and walked down to the street.

He spoke to a rickshaw-wala, and climbed in behind him. The cycle rickshaw began to move.

Mayaram threw away his cigarette and hopped onto his bicycle. Pedalling slowly, he began to follow the rickshaw, making sure to keep a discreet distance.

They passed through the quiet greenery of Rambagh, over the railway crossing near Victoria Jubilee Hospital, and merged into the crowd around Rambagh Gate. The rickshaw was moving at an easy pace, and Mayaram had no trouble keeping up with it.

After weaving through the crowds at Pashamwala Bazaar, the rickshaw reached Katda Jaimal Singh junction and stopped. Mayaram got off his bicycle.

Karnail Singh paid the rickshaw-wala and walked off the main road, down a narrow lane. Mayaram, wheeling the cycle along, followed him.

After walking a short distance, Karnail Singh vanished into the doorway of a two-storey building.

Mayaram paused for a second, then moved ahead. He checked the number on the building—428. He propped the cycle against a wall and climbed a couple of steps to the door. There was no doorbell. He rapped at the door with its shackle.

Karnail Singh leaned out of a window on the first floor and looked out into the lane.

"Who is it?" he asked.

"Karnail Singh?" Mayaram said, looking up.

"Yes."

"Can you come down a minute?" Mayaram said in Punjabi. "I need to discuss something with you."

Karnail Singh's head vanished from the window. A moment later, the door opened, and he reappeared on the threshold. He didn't ask Mayaram to come in.

"Who are you?" he asked suspiciously.

"My name is Mayaram. But most people know me as Ustad."

"I don't know you."

"But you know Kartara, right?"

"Kartara who?"

"Kartar Singh Ahluwalia."

Karnail Singh looked at him for a while, his expression growing hostile.

"Let me come in, at least."

Karnail Singh hesitated, then moved aside, creating just enough space for Mayaram to take a couple of steps in from the doorstep.

"Kartara is dead," Mayaram said in a low voice. "They chanted *Bolo Ram* for him a year ago, in jail. That's why I've come."

"You were with him in jail?"

"Yes."

"Whatever you want to say, say it quickly. I don't want to be seen with a jailbird."

"Shall I say it here?"

"Yes."

"At least close the door."

Karnail Singh took a step and slammed the door.

"You had a deal with Kartara," Mayaram said. "I just wanted to know whether you're still interested."

"I don't know anything about you."

"Then see what you can learn. Kartara was a friend of mine. We've worked together. He said you knew a lot of people like me. So ask around. Every child in Punjab has heard of Mayaram Bawa. You'll hear that the Ustad is even more dependable than Kartara. I'll come back on Friday. Find out all you want about me by then. For now, I just want to know whether you're still interested in that deal."

"I'm going to retire in six months," Karnail Singh said, scratching his beard.

"Six months is a long time."

"But—"

"There's no reason to hurry. I'll be back on Friday, same time."

"Not here!" Karnail Singh said sharply. "If you come here again, I'll have you arrested. I can't be seen associating with people like you; I could be ruined. Don't you know what my job is? If anyone even suspects that people like you visit my home—"

"Leave it. Tell me how you want to meet."

"Phone me."

"Where? At the bank?"

"No, idiot ! Here."

"You have a phone?"

"No. There's one at the neighbour's place. Ask for Karnail Singh from next door."

"Give me the number."

Karnail Singh gave him the number. Mayaram found a pencil and wrote it down on a ragged piece of paper.

"All right. I'll call on Friday."

Karnail Singh said nothing.

"Sat Sri Akaal."

No reply.

Mayaram opened the door and walked out. Karnail Singh banged it shut behind him.

Mayaram took his bicycle and walked with it out of the lane. Reaching the bazaar, he got on the cycle and rode on.

Crossing Hall Bazaar, he came out through Hall Gate, and rode across the overbridge at the Railway Station to reach G.T. Road, where he was staying at a cheap hotel close to the station. He'd rented the bicycle from a shop next door. He returned it and went into the hotel.

At the reception desk, he found out that there had been several calls from Karamchand while he was out.

Instead of going to his room, Mayaram settled down in one of the chairs facing the reception desk. He lit a cigarette and began to puff at it thoughtfully.

Five minutes later, the telephone at the reception rang. Mayaram looked up hopefully. The receptionist picked up the call, listened for a few seconds and then, gesturing to Mayaram, put the phone down on the counter.

Mayaram flicked away the cigarette and walked to the counter. He picked up the receiver and said "Hello?"

"Ustadji?" The voice sounded tense.

"Yes," Mayaram said.

"Ustadji, this is Karamchand."

"Go on."

"The bird's about to fly. I think he's on to us."

"You must have gotten careless."

"No, Ustadji, we were—"

"Where is Labh Singh?"

"He's keeping watch."

"Karamchand," Mayaram snapped, "I'll be there right away. Don't let him escape, even if you have to tie him up. If you two let him get away, I'll slit your throats."

"Don't worry, Ustadji, he's not going anywhere."

Mayaram dropped the receiver back in its cradle and rushed out of the hotel.

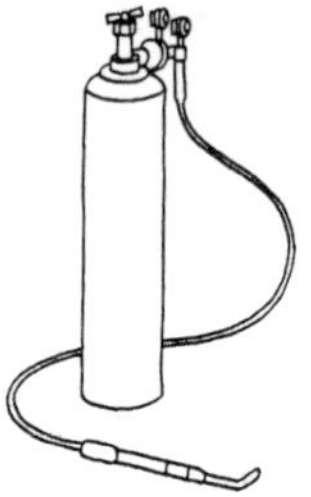

2

VIMAL DREW BACK THE CURTAIN and cautiously looked out.

Outside the bungalow, across the road, a heavyset Sardar stood leaning his flabby body against an electric pole. Earlier, a skinny young man had been with him, but he was nowhere to be seen now.

For the past two days, Vimal had noticed either the big Sardar or the young man loitering around the bungalow. He'd seen them from the room he lived in, above the four-car garage.

The bungalow was in Ajit Nagar, a newly developed area of Amritsar. The houses were big here; the people worked hard and didn't have time for anyone else. There was none of the hustle and bustle of the older parts of Amritsar. It was because the roads were generally so quiet that he'd noticed these two people.

Vimal moved away from the window and went to the far end of the room. There was a suitcase under the bed; he pulled it out. He lifted it onto the bed and dug out a pair of worn bellbottom jeans, a matching jacket with BAN THE BOMB stencilled on the back, and a skin-tight shirt with a wide collar. He found a pair of gold-rimmed glasses with thick lenses and a two-inch-wide iron pendant on a chain. The inscription on the pendant said MAKE LOVE NOT WAR.

He took off his peaked driver's cap and threw

it aside, then took off his uniform. He pulled on the fresh clothes and hung the chain around his neck.

He carefully took off his contact lenses, put them in their little plastic case, squirted in a little liquid, sealed the case, packed it into the suitcase, and put on the glasses. During his Delhi days, he'd gotten used to the contact lenses; it felt a little odd to be wearing glasses again, but he thought they went well with his current hippie getup. With a cap on his head and a pipe in his mouth, no one would realize that this was Surender Singh Sohal of Allahabad, or Vimal Kumar Khanna of Bombay, or Girish Mathur of Madras, or Banwarilal, the tonga-wala from Delhi.

His right hand went nervously to his glasses and took them off. The back of his hand massaged his eyes, and finally the glasses went back onto his nose. He remembered that this was the habitual gesture that had given him away in Delhi.

He took out a cap from the suitcase and put it on. There was a circular patch on the front of the cap embroidered with the word Peace. He put a pipe to his lips and looked at himself in the mirror on the almirah. The result was satisfactory. This same disguise had worked when everyone was looking for him after the fifty lakh robbery in Delhi, and he thought it was good enough for the current situation.

He began to repack the suitcase.

Ever since Allahabad, where his wife Surjeet Kaur and her lover had conspired to get him jailed for embezzlement, fate had been playing cruel games with him. The past year in Amritsar had been very peaceful, but this fat Sardar and his skinny companion smelled of trouble. Either they had recognized him somehow and wanted to turn him in for the reward, or they were up to some game that he didn't know yet. In any case, it was best to slip away quietly.

Here in Amritsar, he was Ramesh Kumar Sharma, driver to Lala Haveli Ram. The Lala lived with his wife, the Sethani—an intoxicating beauty with a sexy figure and a love of stylish clothes and heavy jewellery. She also happened to be twenty years younger than her husband. The Lala had factories in Delhi and Calcutta, and often had to go out of town. There was a cook who worked in the bungalow all day, but who went back to her home on Sultan Wind Road at night. There were two other servants, old and faithful to the Lala, who lived in quarters behind the bungalow. But "Ramesh Kumar Sharma" stayed in a big room over the garage, connected to the main building. When the young Sethani had suggested that he stay there, he'd thought it was because as a driver, he might be summoned at odd hours. The first time the Lala went to Calcutta, however, he realized it was because she wanted him to perform other services besides driving. He also understood why he'd been hired for the job, instead of the other middle-aged, better-qualified candidates.

After some initial hesitation, he'd been fine with the arrangement. The moment Lala Haveli Ram left Amritsar, Vimal would leave his lonely, hard bed and take the Lala's place by the side of the warm, yielding Sethani. Life was wonderful. The Sethani was a caring woman who showered him with the same affection she gave her exotic, pedigreed dog. She fed him the best food and drink, and in the nights, got him to join her in acting out scenes from the Swedish blue films that her husband was addicted to—moves the Lala would never have dreamt that she would enjoy. By day, he was just the driver Ramesh Kumar Sharma; by night, he was "Channa," "Makhna," "Mahi," "Biba," and whatever other pet names she called him.

But perhaps he wasn't fated to live the good life. Perhaps his fate was to wander like a mongrel, kicked off every doorstep.

"If God wills it," he sighed, and closed the suitcase with a heavy heart.

The Sethani was away at a neighbour's. He wanted to slip away before she came back. The relationship between them, though illicit, was strong enough that she would not want to let him go.

He went back to the window. The skinny man had joined the Sardar.

He picked up his suitcase and went to the small kitchen attached to his room. There was a door that opened on to a balcony at the far end, which connected to the first floor of the main building. A narrow corridor led him to a spiral staircase at the rear of the bungalow. He walked down the steps to a small door in the compound wall, opened it, and slipped out.

He stiffened.

A few steps away from him, a man was leaning against the wall, smoking. He gave Vimal an unconcerned look and took another pull from his cigarette. Vimal turned and began to walk away.

"Leaving, Papaji?"

He turned, startled. The man had not moved.

"Did you call me?"

"Yes sir, I called you." The smoker's lips curved into a smile. "I said, Sardar Saheb, leaving so soon?"

"Sardar Saheb?" he stuttered. "Are you crazy? Do I look like a Sardar to you?"

"Yes, you do look like a Sardar to me. I look at you and I see Sardar Surender Singh Sohal in front of me."

Vimal exhaled slowly. "Come here," he said.

The man with the cigarette walked up. He still had a smile on his face.

"Who are you?"

"The name is Mayaram Bawa, but people know me better as Ustad. A big gun like you, maybe you've heard of me?"

"Me, a big gun?"

"In our profession, you're a big gun all right. At such a young age, you've successfully pulled off crimes no one else in India has dared to try. The embezzlement at Eric Johnson in Allahabad; the breakout from jail; Lady Shanta Gokuldas's murder in Bombay; the robbery of fifty-five lakhs in Madras; the sensational fifty lakh bank van hold-up in Delhi. And now I suppose you're here to clean up on Lala Haveli Ram's money."

"You're mistaken."

Mayaram only smiled.

"All right," said Vimal. "Supposing I'm all that you say I am, what then?"

"You want me to tell you everything here?"

"Where else, then?"

"Go back to the bungalow. It's useless to try to run away—you can't, now."

Vimal thought for a few moments, then said, "Let's go."

They went into the bungalow by the same door.

"The two men in the front of the house," Vimal asked, "are they yours?"

"Yes. But they've proved to be failures at keeping a watch over you. The louts don't even know there's a back door to the house. If I hadn't arrived on time, you'd have vanished."

"How did you recognize me?" Vimal asked.

"I've got sharp eyes," Mayaram said, with a touch of pride.

"That you do. But how did you know I was here, in this bungalow in Ajit Nagar?"

"I saw you last Friday at Darbar Saheb. I went early in the morning to bow my head; quite by chance, I noticed you. The moment I saw you, I knew my luck had finally changed. I'd not only found a capable partner, but also solved another big problem."

"What problem?"

"All in good time." By now they were in front of the garage. "You go ahead. I'll bring my friends."

"Okay."

Mayaram walked away. Vimal went back into his room. He took off the hippie clothes and put the driver's uniform back on. He packed the glasses and pipe into the suitcase. He took out his contact lenses. Just as he was fitting them into his eyes, Mayaram and his companions entered.

"Sit down," he told them.

The three sat on the bed.

When Vimal finished with the lenses, he pulled up a chair and sat down, waiting for Mayaram to begin.

"Let me introduce my friends first," Mayaram said. "This is Karamchand," he said, gesturing to the skinny youth on his right. "He's a smart chap. Young, but plucky. He's worked with me before. And this," he continued, gesturing to the fat Sardar to his left, "is Sardar Labh Singh, a.k.a. Matar-Paneer."

"Matar-Paneer?"

"Ever since he was a baby, he's been a big fan of matar-paneer. Lay out the world's greatest feast in front of him, and he'll ask for matar-paneer. Even in jail, he asked for matar-paneer. When he was getting married, the first question he asked his Sardarni was whether she knew how to cook matar-paneer. He can eat an entire goat or half a dozen chickens, but he won't be satisfied unless he gets matar-paneer. Hardly anyone knows him as Labh Singh; they all know him as Matar-Paneer. We've been friends since we were running around in nappies. Everything we've done, honest or illegal, white or black, we've done together. We were in jail together for two years, too."

Vimal looked at Labh Singh "Matar-Paneer." A naïve smile played about his lips, partly hidden by his salt-and-pepper beard. He looked like a cheerful man, but also somewhat dim-witted. The bloodshot eyes, the dark pouches beneath them, the puffy cheeks, and the potbelly all marked him as a man fond of his food and drink. His turban was tied sloppily, as if it had fallen off and been plonked back on. His clothes, too, were dishevelled.

Karamchand, on the other hand, was a dapper and well-dressed young man. He had the sharp features and fair colour of a native Punjabi and seemed up-to-date with the latest fashion. He wore trousers with a narrow fit, and a loose pullover. His long hair was styled in imitation of Sunil Dutt, and he was freshly shaven. His face sparkled with intelligence—no one would have thought he was a criminal.

In contrast to Karamchand and Labh Singh, Mayaram truly looked like a gang leader. Vimal thought the epithet "Ustad" suited him well. He had a wily and alert look, with a face hardened by experience.

"What do we call you?" Mayaram asked. "Sardar Surender Singh Sohal, Vimal Kumar Khanna, Girish Mathur, Banwarilal, Ramesh Kumar Sharma…or something else?"

"Vimal," he said coldly.

"Fine."

"So what's all this about?"

"I have a plan," Mayaram said. "The rest of my life depends on this plan. This is the biggest play I've tried so far, but I guarantee that if I get the right people, nothing can go wrong—we'll clean up at least fifty lakhs."

"Where are these fifty lakh rupees waiting for you?"

"In the vault of Bharat Bank's head office, on Lawrence Road."

"You're planning to get into a bank vault?" Vimal asked, bewildered.

"Yes. I'm the only man who can open this vault for sure. There's no better safecracker in all of India." There was a note of pride in his voice. "I've even worked with Harnam Singh Garewal. He too conceded that I was the best."

Vimal knew the name. Harnam Singh Garewal was a notorious dada. He'd committed countless murders, but had never been caught. The one time they'd arrested him, he'd been acquitted. He'd been involved in everything from smuggling to armed robbery, from drug dealing to pimping. If Garewal thought Mayaram was worth something, then he probably was.

"So why didn't you take this fifty-lakh plan of yours to Garewal?" Vimal asked.

"There's no point," Mayaram said with a sigh. "If I do this with him, he'll take the goat and leave me with the droppings. It won't be an equal partnership; I'll just be a hired hand brought in to open a safe. He'll give me peanuts and swallow all of the loot himself."

"Whereas you want to do everything on your own," Vimal said drily. "You want to swallow all of the loot yourself!"

"I have no such intention," Mayaram said gravely. "Sau rab di, I have no such plans. I only ask for twenty lakhs. The remaining thirty lakhs is for you four to divide amongst yourselves."

"Four?"

"Yes, there's one more person. He has a car workshop near Putli Ghar. He'll be supplying the getaway car, the gas cylinders, the acetylene torch, and all that. If we try to get this stuff anywhere else, someone will get suspicious."

"Who is this man?"

"His name is Guranditta. You'll meet him soon."

"You plan to melt down the vault with an acetylene torch?"

"Yes. There's no other way to open it. There's no way to get the combination for the lock, and the lock is too complicated to take guesses at."

"But vault doors are made of solid steel. Sometimes a few feet thick."

"Don't worry about all that," Mayaram said with complete confidence. "I can open it. I only need some helpers and some inside information."

"How are you going to get the inside information?"

"There's a security guard at the bank named Karnail Singh."

"Why would he tell you anything?"

"He wants money. In six months he has to retire. He has no savings, no other source of income. He'll sell us all the information about the vault and the security."

"How do you know?"

"Through a friend of mine, Kartar Singh Ahluwalia—I met him in jail. He told me about Karnail Singh."

"Is Ahluwalia in this plan as well?"

"No. He's dead. There are only five people involved. First, me, because the plan is mine, and only I can open the vault. Second, Labh Singh, to take shifts with me working the torch. Third, Karamchand, because he has a diploma in electronics. He's the only one who can cut the alarms and the signal wires."

Vimal's impression of Karamchand rose a few notches.

"Fourth, Guranditta," Mayaram continued, "because he's supplying the car and the equipment we need to open the door. And the fifth is you."

"What talent do I have?"

"You're full of talents, but the main talent I've chosen you for is your money."

"What?" Vimal exclaimed, jerking his head up.

"According to my plan, before we can go for the fifty lakhs, we need to spend one lakh."

"But why?"

"Because we'll have to pay Karnail Singh for his information, and it won't be cheap. Kartara figured he'd want at least fifty thousand rupees. The rest we need for the car and the equipment. None of us have money."

"Pull a smaller job, then," Vimal suggested, "to get the money for the big one."

"No," Mayaram shook his head, "I don't want to take the chance. I don't want to risk getting caught on the small job and never getting to the big one. Papaji, this is my last shot. I'm going to use all my skills, all my strength, and all my smarts on this one big job. You know why Kartar Singh Ahluwalia was in jail? He got caught red-handed breaking into a department store—trying to get the money to finance this very job."

"How did he die?"

"It was his time to go, that's all. When Fate is against you, you can't escape. One day in jail, he had a terrible stomach pain. The doctor said it was a stone, and they would have to do a gall bladder operation. Kartara died right there on the operating table."

"Oh."

"And anyway, why do we need to do any small job? Our small job was finding you!"

"But what makes you think that I have money?"

"Don't joke, Papaji! You have the fifty lakh rupees from the Delhi bank van hold-up. Your partners duped you, got you arrested, and escaped with the money. But you broke out of jail. One by one, you bumped off all your partners, and finally you got the loot, too."

"You're mistaken."

"Then where's the money? Your partners are all dead—by your hand—and the cash was never recovered by the police. You must have it."

"Are you an idiot? If I had fifty lakhs, would I be here, driving around for Lala Haveli Ram?"

"Come on. You're not here for the driver's salary, you're here to hide from the police."

"You've got the reason right, but that doesn't mean that I have fifty lakhs. Ustadji, use your head. You just saw me trying to run away from here. Was I going to leave without my money? I only had one suitcase in my hand. Do you think it could hold fifty lakh rupees?"

Mayaram's forehead creased with doubt.

"He must have stashed it in a bank locker somewhere," Karamchand said under his breath. Mayaram looked at Vimal.

"Wrong," Vimal said. "Do you think I'd risk being caught applying for a bank locker?"

Mayaram said nothing.

"And if I really have fifty lakhs, and you're sure of it, then you're the biggest fool on earth."

"What do you mean?"

"You've made this complicated plan to loot fifty lakhs from a bank—so complicated it might even not work out. Who knows whether Karnail Singh will give you anything useful. Who knows whether you'll be able to open the vault. Who knows what else can go wrong! If you're so sure I have fifty lakhs, then why go after the vault at all? Why not just come and grab me by the throat instead? That isn't so difficult."

"Ustadji," Karamchand said after a pause, "he's right."

Mayaram looked at his friends.

"Search him," Labh Singh said.

"Any objections?" Mayaram asked.

"There's nothing to find," Vimal said casually.

"There's no harm in looking."

"I won't let you do it."

"Why not?"

"It's a matter of principle."

"What principle?"

Vimal couldn't think of an answer.

His suitcase was still on the bed. Mayaram picked it up.

"Stop!" Vimal yelled. He lunged out of the chair at Mayaram.

"Labh Singh!" Mayaram growled, "Grab him!"

Labh Singh's flabby bulk moved with surprising speed. His hairy arms wrapped around Vimal and held him with the strength of a bear. Vimal struggled to free himself for a few seconds, then gave up.

Mayaram opened the suitcase and dumped its contents onto the bed.

"Let me go!" Vimal said, helpless. "Ustadji, tell him to let me go."

"Are you going to be trouble?" Mayaram asked him.

"No."

"Labh Singh, let him go."

Labh Singh opened his arms. Vimal collapsed into his chair, then lit a cigarette.

Mayaram searched carefully through the clothes and other articles from the suitcase. All ordinary stuff—nothing unusual. He turned to his companions with a perplexed look.

No one said anything.

He began to put everything back into the suitcase. Suddenly he stiffened, then turned towards Vimal.

"Where are the clothes you were wearing just now?" he asked. "They aren't in the suitcase."

"They're in the wardrobe, but the contents of their pockets are here in my uniform," Vimal tried desperately. "Search me if you like."

Mayaram looked at the wardrobe, and walked towards it.

"I'm telling you, there's nothing there!" Vimal said sharply.

Mayaram ignored him. He opened the wardrobe door and took out the jacket and the bellbottom jeans. Putting his hands into the pockets, he pulled out ten bundles of hundred-rupee notes.

"Wahe Guru!" Vimal murmured. "As You will it."

Mayaram began counting the notes.

"Only ten notes short of a lakh," he said when he was finished.

No one said anything.

"Is this from the bank van hold-up?" he asked Vimal.

Vimal nodded.

"Where's the rest of it?"

"The crocs ate it," Vimal said.

"What do you mean?"

"How do you think I escaped from Tihar Jail after I was arrested for the robbery? The people who got me out took the loot."

"Oh. Then how did you get this money?"

"They let me keep this much."

"All right then. For now we have enough to start. Don't worry—you won't lose this money. You'll get ten lakhs for this one."

"I don't want ten lakhs. I don't even want this one lakh."

"What do you mean?"

"Take the money and stop hounding me. You only needed me for the money—now you have it. Go ahead, finish the job with the people you know well and count me out. Consider this money a bribe to keep your mouth shut about me."

"Impossible. I've told you almost everything about our plan. With one phone call to the police, you could get Karnail Singh into trouble and ruin everything for us."

"Why would I do that?"

"Any number of reasons. The biggest is your one lakh that I'm holding in my hand. Look, brother, we're all cut from the same cloth. We don't betray you, you don't betray us. Besides, you're a very capable man. It's our good fortune to have the chance to team up with a professional criminal of your calibre, with your intelligence and your daring."

"You're wrong about me. I'm none of those things, and whatever crimes I've committed, I've committed because circumstances forced me to."

"Maybe so. Despite all that, you've committed them. This time, try doing something of your own free will."

"So you won't leave me alone?"

"Not a chance."

"Okay," Vimal said finally. "But if I'm a part of the team, I want to have a hand in the planning. I don't want to get caught because of some stupid mistake you make. If any of you are caught, you'll get short sentences. But my police record is so long that I'll go straight to the gallows."

"What do you want?"

"First of all, I want to know why exactly you're sure that the vault will have at least fifty lakhs. And even if it does, how come you get a twenty lakh share? Why not split it equally, five ways?"

"The first question first. Karnail Singh himself told Kartara that the vault always holds at least fifty lakhs, but the day we hit it, it might have sixty, seventy, eighty, even a crore. Fifty lakhs is guaranteed, but we might even get one and a half or twice that. As for your second question, I want twenty lakhs because the plan is mine, the research is mine, and no one but me can get into the vault."

"I could just as well say that without my money, you couldn't get the information from Karnail Singh—and the plan could not succeed."

"But you've been coerced into giving us that money. There's no pressure on me to open that safe."

"That's stupid."

"And then it's possible that we all get equal shares. We might get a crore from the vault. If there's even more than that, then you all could get more than me. I want twenty lakhs. No more, no less."

"I don't like it. Let's do it this way: You get five lakhs for your expertise in opening the safe. I get two lakhs for the one lakh you took from my pocket. After taking out those seven lakhs, we distribute the rest equally."

Karamchand and Labh Singh were looking at Mayaram hopefully. If he agreed to this split, they would get a larger share.

"All right, fine, let's do it your way," Mayaram said offhandedly. "Doesn't make much difference!"

Karamchand and Labh Singh's faces lit up.

Vimal looked at Mayaram. He seemed to have agreed to the split rather too easily.

"One last thing," Vimal said, suddenly harsh. "Remember this: Don't even think about going behind my back. Ever. I've learned a lot of tough lessons in my life. One of them is this: If anyone betrays you, never let them get away with it. You know a lot about me. You yourself just told the story of how I hunted down and killed all my partners from the bank van robbery. Before that, I got Jayashankar, the mastermind of the Anna Stadium robbery, arrested because he thought he could double-cross me the way he'd double-crossed all his other partners. Maybe the same idea has occurred to you. If it has, forget it, otherwise there's no place in the whole world that you'll be safe."

"I have no such intentions," Mayaram said hollowly.

"Good. Mayaram, I've endured a lot of trouble. I've been through such bitter experiences that the pain will follow me even into the next birth. I've seen death up close so many times that I no longer fear it. For me, my life ended the day I escaped from Allahabad Jail. I've been living on borrowed time since then. So the threat to hand me over to the police won't work. What happens if I get caught? I get hanged! The end! It might not even be you—any one of a thousand people could recognize me as a wanted criminal at any time, and bring an end to my story. I can't dodge the police forever; it's just a matter of time. So don't think you hold a sword to my head by threatening to inform the police. I've escaped from jail twice; I can do it a third time. I'll find you in hell, Mayaram Bawa a.k.a. Ustadji. I'm a criminal too, like you. I'm a Punjabi, just like you. Only a dog can sniff out another dog. You may value your life, but I don't."

"Don't worry, Papaji!" Mayaram said in an oily voice. "I swear by God, I have no intention of crossing you."

"Good. Make sure your friends understand that, too."

"Papaji! There's nothing to worry about," Karamchand said.

"We're not that sort of people," Labh Singh said.

"So," Vimal said after a long silence, "do you want to keep the lakh, or should I?"

Mayaram hesitated for a moment and then said, "As you please. It doesn't make a difference now that we're all one group."

"In that case, you keep it."

"No, you take it," Mayaram said, pushing the bundles into Vimal's hands. "I don't need it until Friday. I'll take it then. Who knows, we might get nothing useful out of Karnail Singh and the whole thing will fizzle out before it starts."

Vimal took the money. He couldn't figure out whether his tough talk had made an impression on Mayaram, or whether this was just some ploy.

"And my friend, you said a lot of things about us not crossing you," Mayaram said. "Can we expect the same? Can we be sure that you won't call the police and tell them everything?"

"You can trust me."

"You swear by Wahe Guru?"

"I swear by Wahe Guru."

"Balle!" Labh Singh said. "What are we waiting for? Let's all have a peg!"

He stood up, raised his kurta, and pulled out a three-quarters-full bottle from a fold in his tehmad.

Vimal looked at Mayaram.

"Why not, yaara!" Mayaram said.

Vimal brought out four glasses and a jug of water from the kitchen.

"Chairs!" Labh Singh said, raising his glass.

"And tables!" Karamchand said.

Vimal looked puzzled.

Mayaram looked at Vimal and laughed. "Labh Singh thinks they say *chairs* when they say *cheers*. And tables go with chairs!"

Vimal couldn't help laughing too.

Labh Singh drank about half of the contents of the bottle himself, and the other three drank the rest.

"Wonderful!" Labh Singh said, wiping his moustache after polishing off his last drink. "Let's go now. I know a hotel opposite the bus stand. They have such lovely matar-paneer that you'll be licking your fingers! You'll forget all about butter chicken!"

"I can't come," Vimal said. "You folks go ahead."

"Okay," Mayaram said, rising. "We're off. I'll be meeting you again. The next time, I'll introduce you to our fifth partner."

"Fine."

Everyone shook hands, and Mayaram left with the other two.

Vimal sank down onto the bed, holding his head in his hands, brooding over the new trouble that had found its way to his doorstep.

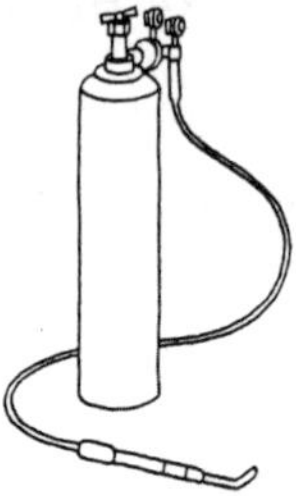

3

Karnail Singh reached his home.

He took off his guard uniform and turban and pulled on a long kurta and pajama. He threw a thick, warm shawl about his shoulders. In the kitchen, he made tea and poured it into a brass tumbler. He sat in the front room with the tumbler. As always, he felt a light pain in his chest. Every evening, by the time he arrived home, tired, the pain would begin. The doctor said it was only a sign of old age, nothing to worry about. But Karnail Singh knew better. He was deathly afraid of the pain. Seven years ago, his wife had complained of a similar chest pain, and had died of it not long after. She'd suffered such a severe heart attack that she hadn't even been able to draw a breath before she was gone. Karnail Singh thought that he too, someday soon, would go out like a fused bulb.

He opened a cupboard and took out a bottle of brandy. Pouring a generous helping into his tumbler, he went back to the diwan. He took a few more sips of the tea.

Today was Friday. Mayaram would be calling any minute now.

The brandy in the tea eased the tightness in his chest, and made him feel better.

When he'd asked around about Mayaram Bawa, he'd found, to his relief, that he was known as a man of his word, just like Kartar Singh Ahluwalia had been. He'd also heard that he was a reputed safecracker, and had recently completed a seven-year sentence.

An image of Mayaram's face came to him.

He knew several criminals who'd spent most of their lives in jail. Not one had come out of jail unchanged; they'd been either broken or hardened. All jailbirds went through this change, mentally and physically. But Mayaram seemed to be the sort of man who could bear any pressure without cracking. He seemed to have emerged from jail the same man he'd been when he went in. Prison had left no mark on him—the solitude had only sharpened his thinking and the hard labour had strengthened his muscles. He seemed to be the sort who'd stop at nothing to get what he wanted, even if he might lose his life in the effort. Karnail Singh felt a sense of relief in dealing with such a man, and not some half-baked hoodlum.

Karnail Singh lived alone in this rented house. When his wife died seven years ago, his only daughter had been twenty years old. He had gotten her married two years later—spent his whole life savings on it, and borrowed quite a bit from a moneylender too. Now he was about to retire, and he would get barely ten thousand from his Provident Fund and Gratuity.

He'd expected to get a lakh from the deal with Kartara. He'd wanted to use the money to go to London, where his daughter had gone a year after her marriage. His son-in-law had opened a Punjabi restaurant in Southall. He would go stay with them, get himself treated at a good hospital, and live the rest of his days in peace. But he couldn't do it with the ten thousand he'd get when he retired. That was why he'd dealt with Kartara, but the deal hadn't worked out. Now, perhaps, it would work out with Mayaram.

Someone rapped the shackle on the door below.

Karnail Singh put the empty tumbler on the floor under the diwan, walked to the window, and looked out. A ten-year-old boy was standing there.

"What is it, boy?" he asked in Punjabi.

"Tayaji," the boy said, looking up, "there's a phone for you."

"Wait, wait. I'm coming."

He picked up his turban, set it on his head, and walked down to the door and across to the neighbour's house.

The receiver was lying to the side of the phone. He held it to his ear and said "Hello?"

"Karnail Singh?" the voice at the other end said.

"Aaho."

"It's Friday. I told you I'd call."

Karnail Singh did not answer. He looked to see if there was anyone around. The room was empty, but he could hear voices from the adjoining room.

"I'm going to Darbar Saheb to pay my respects." Without waiting for Mayaram to answer, he set the receiver back in its cradle.

He went back home, put on a sweater, locked the door, and walked out.

Darbar Saheb was close enough to reach on foot.

At the entrance, he looked around. Mayaram was nowhere to be seen.

He deposited his chappals at the shoe-stand, washed his hands and feet, and went up the steps, praying to Wahe Guru.

He made one complete round of the sarovar, walking on the cool white marble path. Back at the entrance, he paused.

He still didn't see Mayaram.

He crossed the bridge over the sarovar and entered the Gurudwara. As always, the Guru Granth Saheb was being chanted inside. He gave a coin from his pocket as an offering, bowed at the threshold, accepted the prasad, and returned after making a circumbulation.

Mayaram was sitting on the entrance steps.

Their eyes met for just an instant, then Karnail Singh looked away. He retrieved his chappals from the shoe-stand and sat down on a bench.

Mayaram got up, got his own shoes from the stand, and sat down next to him. He neither looked at Karnail Singh nor tried to talk to him.

"I'm going to say this only once," Karnail Singh murmured, his head bent. "So listen carefully. Don't try to argue—you'll be wasting your time. Once I retire, I'm leaving this country for good and going to London. My passport and other papers are ready. I have no relatives here. So you're in no position to threaten me. If you so much as look at me the wrong way, I'll have you arrested. You're a known criminal. All I need to do is tell them that you're planning a heist, and you'll be in for good. I'm a security guard at the bank, and you're a thief. There's not a single black mark on my thirty-year record, and you've been to jail five times. The police will take my word over yours."

"What do you want?" Mayaram asked, pulling out a sock from one shoe and shaking the dust out of it. "What's your price?"

There were many people walking around, but no one seemed to pay them any attention. They were just two devotees visiting the gurudwara, sitting by chance on the same bench, putting on their footwear.

"One lakh," Karnail Singh said, slapping the soles of his chappals together. "In cash. Advance."

"How much will be inside the vault?"

"Fifty lakhs minimum. There's no maximum. It could be anything."

"And you're satisfied with one lakh? Why don't you partner up with us? Help us out, and we'll cut you an equal share of the loot."

"I don't want a share. I want one lakh. In cash. Advance. I don't trust you thieves, and won't have anything to do with you. I don't want to be seen with you. There'll be a huge commotion after the robbery. The security guards will be first suspects, including me. I won't risk my neck."

"What do we get in exchange for the one lakh?"

"The wiring plan for the alarm systems. The locations of the alarm bells. The timetable of the guards' rounds and routes. All the details about the doors and windows. The thickness of the vault door. A plan of the whole building. Kartar Singh must have told you what you'd get from me."

"He did," Mayaram said, pulling on a sock. "But he didn't tell me that your demand would be so high. He said you'd ask for forty or fifty thousand."

"One lakh. In cash. Advance."

"Do I need to count it out into your palm?" Mayaram put on his other sock.

"No. I'll give you the address of a man. Give him the money, and give me the receipt. For a ten percent commission, he will give me the value in pounds in London."

"What if he doesn't give you the pounds later?"

"That's not your headache. The day you give me the receipt for the one lakh, your work will be done."

"But one lakh is too much, really too much..."

"I told you, don't bother to argue," Karnail Singh said roughly. He was searching for an imaginary nail poking through his chappal.

"Fifty thousand now, in cash. The rest after the job is done." Mayaram pushed a foot into a shoe. If the old guy agreed to this, he'd never find them after the job.

"No." Karnail Singh shook his head, still looking down.

"But we don't have that much money," Mayaram said, tying his laces. "We can pay you double or triple after the job is done. Take sixty thousand, that's the maximum we can pay now."

Karnail Singh didn't bother to answer. He put both slippers on.

"Seventy," Mayaram said.

Karnail Singh stood up. He seemed in a hurry to go.

"Eighty," Mayaram said, quickly tying the laces on his other shoe. "And if that's not enough, to hell with you."

"Ninety," Karnail Singh said. "Take down the name and address of the man you have to give the money to. Satyapal Gupta. House number 40, Rani ka Bagh. Telephone me after you have the receipt."

Without waiting for Mayaram to answer, he strode away.

Mayaram stood up quietly, watching him go.

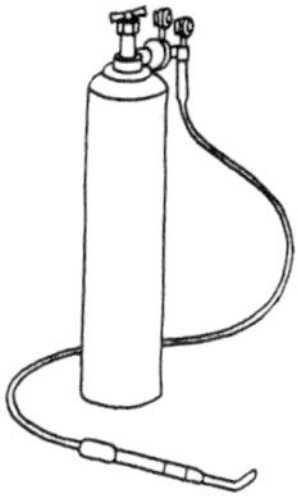

4

Over the next few days, Vimal did not see Mayaram, Labh Singh, or Karamchand tailing him, but there was another man he noticed several times. This man was about forty years old, with a broad forehead and a well-groomed moustache. He was always dressed in an open-collared shirt, tight-fitting pants made of some strange fabric, and a tweed coat. Once or twice, he had a muffler around his neck. Only the muffler seemed to be new and clean.

Though Mayaram hadn't introduced Guranditta yet, Vimal was sure that this was him. It didn't seem logical that Mayaram would hire yet another person to keep an eye on him.

Vimal had no intention of slipping away, so he didn't really care whether anyone was watching him.

He had been to Lawrence Road one evening to have a look at Bharat Bank. What he'd seen of the security made him think it would be impossible to even get close to the building. He wondered how Mayaram could be so sure of getting in and opening the vault.

By now Lala Haveli Ram had returned from his trip. This meant that Vimal was usually free at night. The Lala would drive to the Lumbsdon Club in the evenings with his wife. If by chance the Lala was busy,

Vimal would have to ferry the ape's angel to the club himself.

One night, about ten o'clock, Mayaram came to meet him.

"Come, let me give you a tour of the bank," he said, after they shook hands.

"I've seen it already," Vimal said. "Ustadji, forget about getting into that bank. It's out of the question. It isn't even possible to get close to the building at night."

"Come on anyway. Take another look."

Rather reluctantly, Vimal agreed to go. They got into a rickshaw and set off.

Vimal couldn't see the man with the muffler anywhere. He was now certain that the man was Mayaram's partner: Vimal didn't need to be tailed if Mayaram was with him.

"Did you talk to the security guard?" Vimal asked.

"Yes. That bastard was demanding a lakh," Mayaram said, scowling. "I got him down to ninety thousand, finally."

"Waste of money. His inside information won't be any use if you can't even get into the bank. The security there is really tight. What do you intend to do, shoot all the guards and walk in the front door? Climb up a pipe? Or are you going to fly in?"

"Fly in," Mayaram said calmly.

"What do you mean?" Vimal said, incredulous.

"You'll understand soon. For now, just get a lay of the land."

"But—"

"Look, you've said you don't care about your life, but I care about mine. Personally, I'm quite fond of living. I'm forty-five years old and I've done five stints in jail already. If I wind up there again, I'll die there. Just thinking about that place makes me shiver. But I need to make one more attempt to get my hands on some money. I'm a born thief, after all... How do you expect me to change? I've always lived the good life; I can't imagine doing a menial job. What would it get me? Dry roti two times a day, when I've always eaten the richest ghee. Good drink, good women, good food… How else am I supposed to get all this, if my only talent is opening safes? Papaji, I've already told you, this is the last gamble of my life. I want to live out the rest of my days on the money from this job. Now you tell me: If I wasn't absolutely sure about it, do you think I'd attempt it?"

Vimal had to admit that Mayaram had a point.

The rickshaw reached Lawrence Road. They got down a fair distance away from the bank, lit cigarettes, and walked on.

The road was almost deserted at that hour. A few restaurants were still open, but there were hardly any vehicles parked outside.

The part of Lawrence Road on which the vast four-storey Mehta House was situated was bereft of shops, so there was hardly anyone about. To the left of the bank, separated by a street about twenty feet wide, was another building of about the same height that housed some offices and residential flats. To the rear was another street, narrower than Lawrence Road, with a few bungalows and empty plots. To the right of the bank was an office building occupied by a transport company. This building was separated from Mehta House by a fifty-foot-wide street. The only source of light here was a single bulb fixed to the outer wall of the transport company office, about fifteen feet above the ground. The bulb had a shade over it that focused the light down onto the street.

"There's another bulb on the far side of the building," Mayaram explained. "But it's fused. We'll have to take out this one, too, and then the road will be dark."

Vimal said nothing. He was looking at the huge compound in front of Mehta House, where several security guards were on duty. Other guards were on patrol around the building.

They paused for a moment in the front of the bank, walked on, and, after a while, turned back.

"Kartara told me that there are two types of alarms in the bank," Mayaram said in a low voice. "The alarms on the building go off if anyone tries to break in. The alarm on the vault door only goes off at the nearest police station. So, even if someone gets in, he'll notice nothing when he touches the vault, until the police are on him. We need to cut both these alarms."

"How?" Vimal asked.

"Using the information that Karnail Singh gives us. He'll provide a complete wiring plan of the building. The wire to the police station goes through a P. & T. cable line. He'll give us the cable route and the pair number for the alarm wires."

"Even if you cut the alarms, how will you bypass all these guards and get into the building?"

"I told you. By flying."

"Don't make jokes."

"We get in through the transport company building. It doesn't have a guard. There are so many of them around the bank, and they're so rigorous, the transport company doesn't even bother to have a chowkidar. We can get into that building very easily. I've seen the lock on the gate there—it's an ordinary lock. I'll make a key for it. From the fourth floor of that building, we can get across to the fourth floor of Mehta House. If it's a dark night, the guards won't be able to see a ladder going across overhead even if they look up. I don't expect them to look up, anyway. They're so confident of their arrangements that they don't believe anyone would ever try to get into the bank."

"Hmm."

"There's another narrow alley on the other side of the transport company building. There's a door there which leads to the office. It has a double lock. I was here the day before yesterday; I stuck a soft iron slip into the keyholes and turned it. The levers of the locks made impressions on the iron, which I used to make two keys. Come on, let's check whether the keys work."

Vimal hesitated, then followed him.

They went into the alley to the right of the building. It was deserted.

"Stay here," Mayaram said. "If you see anyone, give me a warning."

Vimal nodded. Mayaram walked up the two steps to the door.

A couple of minutes later, he was back.

"Let's go," he said.

"What happened?"

"One of the keys is first class. The lock opened in two seconds. The other one worked, too, but it wasn't smooth enough—I'll have to work with it, shouldn't be a problem. The next time, the other lock will open in two seconds, too."

"Hmm. Now what?"

"We're done, let's go."

They began to look for a rickshaw.

"I've looked into this transport company thoroughly. Their truck to the South is scheduled only once a week, on Wednesday. That means if you book something for Madras on a Thursday, it will be lying around in their godown till the next Wednesday, when it will get loaded into their truck and begin its journey. I also found out that the packages for Madras are stored on the fourth floor of the building."

"How does all this help?"

"It helps a lot. We'll pack the gas cylinder, acetylene torch, folding ladder, gas mask, and all that, and book it for Madras. That way, we won't have to carry it up to the fourth floor; it'll be ready for us when we come here."

"That's good!" Vimal said. He was beginning to think that Mayaram might actually have a chance.

They found a rickshaw and got into it.

"I'm getting off at the next corner," Mayaram said. "I'll be back tomorrow for the money. There's a little hitch because Karnail Singh asked for more than expected, but I think we'll make it."

"All right," Vimal said.

"And Papaji, don't worry about your money. You'll get it back."

"Where do you live?"

"At the Grand Hotel. Why?"

"Just wanted to know. But where are you from really?"

"Stop here, boy," Mayaram told the rickshaw-wala. To Vimal, he said, "I'll meet you tomorrow."

He got down from the rickshaw. Vimal opened his mouth to say something, then changed his mind. He waved at Mayaram. The rickshaw began moving again.

Mayaram walked away swiftly, down the empty road.

Overleaf: Raja Pocket Books Advertisement for "The 102nd novel in Surender Mohan Pathak's 'Sunil' series: *Stop Press*".

सुरेन्द्र मो
सुन
का 102वां

पाठक

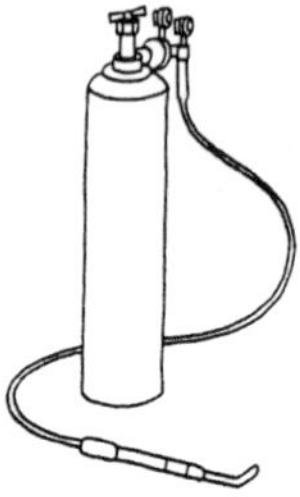

5

On the platform, Mayaram walked along the entire length of the train, looking through each window.

The bogie in which he found Karnail Singh was otherwise empty. Karnail Singh was sitting cross-legged, reading an Urdu newspaper. Mayaram coughed softly. Karnail Singh raised his head but showed no reaction to Mayaram. He looked past him, as if Mayaram were transparent, and then looked back down at his paper.

Mayaram moved away from the window. He stood on the platform, waiting for the signal-down.

He'd called Karnail Singh the night before to tell him that he'd deposited the ninety thousand with Satyapal Gupta and gotten the receipt. In reply, Karnail Singh had only said that he was going to meet his friend in Batala tomorrow on the morning train, and had cut the line.

Mayaram had reached the station a few minutes before the train's departure time.

It was Sunday. Perhaps that was why the creaking passenger train had hardly any travellers. The train's last stop was Pathankot, and most of its passengers were weekday commuters.

The signal turned green. The guard waved the green flag. The train pushed forward tiredly, as if unwilling to go on.

There were still no other passengers in Karnail Singh's bogie. As the train picked up speed, Mayaram jumped in.

Karnail Singh looked at him as if he were an unwelcome visitor. He folded up the paper and set it aside.

"Ridiculous," Mayaram said, sitting down next to him with a thump. "This is a horrible place to meet."

"This place is fine," Karnail Singh said coldly. "I don't want anyone to see me with the likes of you."

"What if this bogie hadn't been empty?"

"I know this train; it's always nearly empty on holidays."

"But there are a few passengers. Someone might have sat in here."

"Even if he did, he would have got down at Verka or Kathu Nangal. If he didn't, I'd have gotten off."

"All right, Badshaho," Mayaram said, defeated. "Whatever makes you happy."

"Give me the receipt."

Mayaram handed him the slip of paper.

"I know Satyapal Gupta's signature," Karnail Singh said. He inspected the slip carefully. Finally satisfied, he nodded, folded up the receipt, and put it into an inner pocket of his waistcoat.

"All fine?" Mayaram asked.

"Yes."

"Start your story, then."

"Listen," Karnail Singh said severely. "I'll explain this only once. If you have any doubts, ask me immediately. If you think you can't remember something, write it down. After today, I won't meet you. I don't want to see your face or have anything to do with you anymore. I'm warning you: After today, don't call me, don't come to my home, don't call out to me in the bank, don't wave to me in the street. If you try anything like that, I'll report you to the police immediately. I don't want to know how and when you intend to use the information I'm giving you. And don't expect any other help from me. If you try to rob the bank while I'm on my shift, I'll do my duty without any hesitation. And I don't think I need to tell you what my duty is.

"I'm not your partner. I have no part in your plan, so don't get any filmi ideas about me giving you the keys, or cutting the alarm wires for you, or letting you go if I catch you. Don't even think about it."

"Understood."

Karnail Singh took out a long envelope from his waistcoat. He carefully extracted a dirty sheet of paper from it and dropped it onto Mayaram's lap.

Mayaram unfolded it slowly and spread it out. There was a complicated mess of lines on it. He realized this was a detailed map of Mehta House. It had the location of the front, side, and rear entrances, approach roads, the layout of the compound, the windows, and the plan of each floor. There were markings to indicate the size of each feature.

"Wherever you seen an 'A' on the map," Karnail Singh said, "that's an alarm bell. There are four of them, one on each corner of the building, thirty feet above the ground. There's one more alarm, linked to the vault door, which rings directly at the police station. There are at least six security staff always on duty—even at noon. There are several entrances to the building, but only one way into the vault, and that is a flight of stairs going down to the basement. The lights in the building are kept on twenty-four hours a day. The vault is sixty feet from the foot of the stairs in the basement. The walls and ceiling of the vault are made of concrete reinforced with steel, and there's a layer of steel on the inside. That means it's impossible to drill through the walls or roof. The only way to get into the vault is through the door. But perhaps you've thought of some other route."

Mayaram didn't say anything. He was registering every word.

Karnail Singh paused for a few seconds and then said, "Not all the guards are armed, but during the night shifts, at least three of them are. All of the armed guards are excellent marksmen and ruthless by nature."

"Don't bother about that. Tell me about the security setup at night."

"Okay. Usually, the vault closes at six p.m. and the bank closes by seven. While closing down, the entire building is checked, and double locks are put on all the doors. No one stays inside. The guards are posted outside, and they patrol around the bank all night."

"What do you mean by double locks?"

"All entrances to the building have two locks each. One key remains with the security-in-charge, the other with a bank official. It takes both keys to open any door, and a different official is entrusted with the keys every day. There are duplicate keys, but they're kept at two other branches, which means you'd have to break into two other banks to get them. Even if you attack the security-in-charge and get one key, it'll be impossible to get the other, because you won't know who has it that day. The decision as to which official will keep the key on any given day is made by the authorities just five minutes before the bank closes. Even the security-in-charge doesn't know who has it. He only finds out the next morning when that official shows up to open the doors.

"What sort of locks are these?"

"Very strong, very reliable. Foreign-made, imported. None of them has fewer than nine levers."

"Hmm. Go on."

"I've already told you that no one stays in the building after it's locked, so there's no one you can persuade or threaten into opening the doors from the inside. All the doors and windows in the building are rigged to the alarms. The bells, as I've already told you, are thirty feet above the ground—out of reach. The vault door weighs five tons and is two and a half feet thick. It has a combination lock, but it's not a fixed combination. The numbers used to close the door in the evening are the same ones required to open it the next day."

"Do they really change the numbers every day?"

"I don't know. Only the managers decide that. Usually, the person who closes the vault isn't given the keys to the entrances, and the one who has the keys knows nothing about the combination. So the responsibility for security is distributed."

"Go on."

"The vault alarm is connected to the bell at the police station by a wire routed through a P. & T.

department cable. I've drawn the path of that cable in pencil on the map, and also marked the colour code of the wire so you can identify it."

"The bank employees must have to open the vault during the day. Shouldn't there be a switch, then, to turn the alarm off and on again?"

Karnail Singh laughed. "There is. But the switch is inside the vault."

"How's that possible? How do they turn it off before they open the door in the morning?"

"They can't. Every day, when they open the vault at ten, the bell rings at the police station. Before they open it, they telephone the police to notify them. The bank closes at three on Saturday and opens on Monday morning at ten, which means there's a gap of forty-three hours. The patrols start at dusk and go on till sunrise. There's a big room near the gate of the compound; that's where the security chief's office is, and also where the guards rest when they're not on patrol duty. There are at least four guards on patrol at all times, and they work in six-hour shifts. It's useless to hope for any slackness—they're very disciplined. They're well-paid, duty-bound, honest people."

"Except you." It escaped out of Mayaram's mouth before he could stop it.

Karnail Singh glared at him. Controlling himself, he said, "Stick to the topic. Don't try to be smart."

"All right, all right."

"There's another button in the security office which connects to the vault alarm. There's at least one man on duty there all night. Every time the guards complete one round of their patrol, they signal the man inside with a buzzer. He has strict instructions that if the buzzer doesn't go off on time, he is to immediately trigger the police station alarm. The point of all this is that capturing the guards on patrol will get you nowhere."

"Keep talking. And we're nearly at the station, so wag your tongue faster. You have to give me ninety thousand rupees worth of information."

"Here's the part that's really worth the money: the patrol timetable."

"Tell me."

"The first patrol starts twenty-three minutes after the bank closes. The next one starts twenty-four minutes later; the next, fifty-three minutes after that. Then there's a gap of half an hour, after which the whole order is reversed. By that I mean there's another fifty-three minutes before the fourth round starts, then twenty-four minutes before the fifth round, and then twenty-three minutes before the sixth round. Then the whole sequence is repeated, till dawn. I've written it all down on the back of the map. After every round, the main entrance to the bank is checked. There's a peephole in the door, through which you can see the main hall. I already told you that the lights inside the building are never turned off. Through this peephole, you can see the stairs to the basement—the only way to get to the vault."

"What else is there in the basement?"

"Nothing, just the vault."

"How do they get fresh air down there?"

"There's an air duct, but if you think you can get in through that, forget it. It's impossible."

"Hmm," he said, and began studying the map. Karnail Singh waited, silent, next to him.

The train stopped at Verka Station.

Mayaram folded the map and put it in his pocket. Two beggar girls got into the bogie and sat down on the floor close to the door.

Mayaram lit a cigarette. Karnail Singh made a face. Mayaram got up, sat by a window, and exhaled smoke.

The train began to move again. After it passed the outer signal, Mayaram took out the map again, spread it on his lap, and began to study it closely. He took a piece of paper and a pencil from his pocket and made a few calculations. He knew he had to get everything straight right here and now. Karnail Singh was stubborn; when he'd said he would have nothing to do with Mayaram after this, he'd meant it. Trying to contact him again would create trouble. He turned his attention back to the vault door.

Two and a half feet thick!

His mouth felt dry. Was he fooling himself, or could he really get the door open? No way he could blow it open. To blast a door that thick would require so much explosive that the entire building was liable to be blown up, and the people inside with it.

No. There was only one way—the one he'd thought of from the beginning. It would have to be melted open.

But melting a hole through a wall of steel thirty inches thick was no joke. He checked his calculations. With a thirty-two-hundred-degree flame, it would take five or six hours to burn a hole big enough for a man to get through. The flame would also use up the oxygen in the surrounding air. To breathe comfortably, they'd have to take oxygen tanks. Even after the opening was made, the door would be red hot. They would have to wait quite a while for it to cool down.

He felt the train slowing down. He folded the map carefully and put it in his pocket. He tore the piece of paper he'd been writing on into tiny bits and scattered it out the window.

The train stopped at Kathu Nangal Station.

Mayaram got up from his seat and, without looking at Karnail Singh, got off the train.

There was a highway near the station. He caught a bus back to Amritsar.

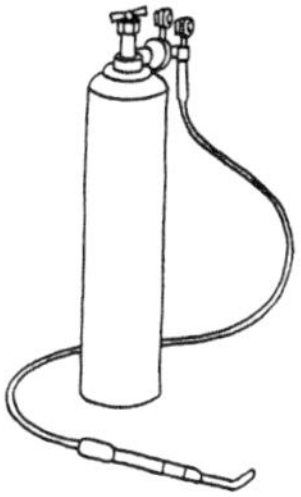

6

THE OFFICE OF THE MOTOR GARAGE was a cabin made of peeling wood panels. Behind the table, on a dilapidated chair, sat the man with the tight-fitting trousers, the tweed coat, and the muffler. Mayaram had introduced him as Guranditta, so Vimal's guess had been proven right.

Labh Singh "Matar-Paneer" sat quietly off to one side on two tyres. To Vimal, it looked like he'd had a couple of pegs already. Once, when he changed position, his kurta shifted a bit, and Vimal caught a glimpse of a bottle of whiskey tucked into his tehmad.

Karamchand sat on a stool next to Guranditta, his expression serious.

Vimal was sitting on the edge of a long seat that had been scavenged from a bus, which he'd dragged up to the desk.

The last chair was occupied by Mayaram, who had spread out Karnail Singh's map on the table.

"Have you studied the wiring for the police station alarm?" Mayaram asked Karamchand.

"Yes," he said briefly.

"Can you do the job?"

"What sort of question is that?" Karamchand said. "What else am I here for?"

Mayaram looked at him. "Vah, vah!" he said appreciatively.

"It appears from the map," Karamchand explained, "that the wire from the vault joins up with the underground P. & T. cable within the Mehta House compound. The wire separates from the cable within the police station, and even then it's encased in an iron pipe. What I mean to say is that the wire can't be cut at either end—otherwise it would have been easy. So we'll have to do this the hard way—dig up the cable in between. There are a lot of telephone lines routed through Lawrence Road. There must be at least a hundred wire pairs in that cable. We'll have to identify the pair that Karnail Singh marked, cut it, repair the cable, and then bury it again."

"And you'll do all this out in the open?"

"Yes, but it doesn't matter. Telephone cables get damaged all the time. I'm sure you've seen telephone department workers put up their canvas tents on the road to dig up and repair cables. Ever paid any attention to them?"

"No," Mayaram said.

"No one does."

"But what if someone from the telephone department notices?"

"I don't think that's likely. Cable repair is very common in big cities. No one will think anything of it."

"Hmm." Mayaram didn't look very confident.

"Don't worry about it, Ustadji," Karamchand said reassuringly, "This is my job. Leave it to me."

"All right."

"But you'll have to arrange for my equipment in advance."

"What equipment?"

"A tent, digging tools, lead and paper sleeves for the wires, bitumen compound, some tools—pliers, that sort of thing."

"I'll take care of it," Guranditta said.

"When will you do it?" Mayaram asked Karamchand. "In broad daylight?"

"After dark," Karamchand said, "Eight o'clock should be fine."

"Won't people get suspicious, seeing government employees working so late?"

"People will be happy! They'll be pleased that after the Emergency, P. & T. employees have become so devoted to their work," Karamchand grinned. "But seriously, cable repair work goes on all the time, even at night."

"And how long will it take?"

"If I don't have to do a very clean job, two and a half hours should be enough."

"In that case, start at seven instead of eight. If you run late, it will affect the rest of the plan."

"Okay."

"Have you arranged for the welding equipment?" Mayaram asked Guranditta.

"All done. I've packed the gas cylinders and the rest of the equipment in wooden boxes," Guranditta said. "I've also packed a gas mask, a fire extinguisher, and a sixty-foot folding aluminium ladder. I'll get all this to the transport company office on Friday morning and book it for Madras."

"Excellent!"

"So when you do plan to do the job?" Vimal asked.

"Saturday night," Mayaram said. "There are six days left. In the meantime, we'll make sure that the patrol schedule is exactly as Karnail Singh told us."

"Any other preparations?"

"Karamchand is making two wireless sets. We'll use them to communicate between the transport company godown and the bank building after we get in. If something goes wrong—pray it doesn't—they'll be crucial for our escape."

"Very good," Vimal nodded.

"Besides that, I think everyone ought to have watches—we'll synchronize them so that we can keep track of the patrols down to the second. Labh Singh and I don't have watches, so we'll have to buy two good ones."

"All right."

"We should have a gun or two," Guranditta said.

"I don't think so," Mayaram said. "If we can't get in, the guns will be no use anyway. If the guards notice us after we're in, we'll be like birds in a cage. It's impossible to escape from there; even a machine gun wouldn't be enough against all those guards. Shooting at the guards wouldn't help us escape, it would just double our jail terms. It'd be armed dacoity, not just stealing. We'd be tried as killers. If anyone has a gun, tell me now. I don't want anyone to bring one along and shoot somebody by mistake."

No one said anything.

"Vimal?"

"I don't even have a pen knife, let alone a gun."

"All right. As I've already said, we'll get to the roof of the bank by climbing across a ladder from the fourth-floor window of the transport company building. The bank has a sloping roof, but there's a six-inch wide skirting around the edges. Someone has already considered the possibility of intruders trying to break into the bank from the neighbouring building, since it's so close. That's why they've rigged all the fourth-floor windows of Mehta House with alarms. Now they seem sure that even if someone reaches the roof, they won't be able to get in."

"But we will?"

"Yes. The plan is that once we're on the roof, Karamchand and I will cut the wires to the four alarm bells on the corners. The bells are thirty feet above the ground, which means they're about twenty-five feet below the roof. I'll have to lower Karamchand by rope to get to the wires. Then we can open the window of the bank and get the ladder into it. That's how the rest of you—and the equipment—will get into the bank."

"But won't they see us on the ladder? Won't they see the ladder itself?"

"No chance. There's a new moon on Saturday. It's winter; it gets foggy most nights. The ladder won't be visible from the street below, and we're going to keep careful track of the patrol timetable. We'll set up the ladder only after the guards have passed. So we don't need to worry about being seen. What we really need to be careful about is being *heard*. Someone could hear us even if he isn't directly below us in the street. So when we're carrying the gas cylinders and all that across the ladder, we have to be extremely careful. If anything slips out of our grasp and falls, it'll make enough noise to ruin the game."

Mayaram stopped to see the effect his words were having, and then continued. "Once we're in the building, we'll climb down the steps to the ground floor. We'll have to wait for the right moment to cross the hall so that we're not seen through the peephole. We can't depend on guesswork for this part—we need to be sure the guards aren't about to finish their patrol and check. This is where the wireless sets come in. The patrols will be visible from the transport company window. We'll have to leave one person there. He'll tell us when we can go down into the basement safely."

"Who'll stay behind?" Vimal asked.

"Karamchand. He'll be exhausted after hanging from the rope and cutting the alarm wires; he won't be any use to us after that. He'll go back to the transport company building and pull the ladder in after we've crossed over."

"Will he be able to pull the ladder in alone?"

"It's an aluminium ladder. It's quite light."

"I see."

"Karnail Singh demanded too much money. I had planned to use the rest of it to buy a secondhand car and a van. If we had two vehicles, we could have gotten out of the state easily, but now it won't be possible. We can't even afford to buy one. But we'll have to make the best of it."

"We can't do it without a car!" Vimal protested.

"We'll have to make do with the vehicles that come to Guranditta's workshop for repairs—there's no other option. He'll make sure that we have one car and one pickup van on Saturday. That changes the plan, though—we won't be able to get out of the state immediately after the heist. We can't take Guranditta's cars with us, because we have to return them to the garage by morning. But I guess that should be all right."

"No problem," Labh Singh said carelessly.

"So that's the whole plan," Mayaram said. His sharp eyes stopped at each one of them in turn. "Any questions?"

No one said anything.

Vimal cleared his throat. "I don't have a question," he said. "But I do have a suggestion."

Everyone turned to him.

"What?" Mayaram asked.

"Labh Singh's tehmad won't work for this little excursion."

"What do you mean?" Labh Singh sputtered.

"You might trip on it. If that happens while walking across the ladder, you'll go down fifty-five feet to the road. This job requires tight-fitting clothes."

"What do you want me to do? Wear pants?"

"Yes."

"Listen, brother. I've been wearing a tehmad since I was born. Not once have my feet gotten tangled in it."

"There's a first time for everything."

"Don't you worry about me. If you really insist, I'll take off the tehmad when the time comes and wrap it around my neck. I can't wear pants."

"Another thing. You seem to be drunk all the time. That's going to make you careless."

Labh Singh's face went red to the ears. He opened his mouth to respond, but Mayaram said, "All right. Labh Singh won't drink on Saturday."

"But—" Labh Singh started to protest.

"Oye, Labh Singh," Mayaram said, "Do this for me, you lout!"

"All right, all right," said Labh Singh. "But Ustadji, tell him that it's only young cockerels like him who lose their senses when they drink. Me, I get smarter and more alert."

"Sardar Saheb," Vimal said as pleasantly as he could, "please don't take it the wrong way. I'm only saying it for everyone's safety."

"Okay then. If it's a problem, I won't drink that day."

"Thank you."

"But the ban is for Saturday, isn't it? Not for today?"

"I'm not saying there's a *ban*," said Vimal. "I was just saying—"

"Then what are we waiting for? Let's all have a peg!" Labh Singh pulled the bottle from his tehmad and thumped it on the table.

"Excellent!" Guranditta said. "Labh Singh, just for this, I'm going to order you the best matar-paneer you've eaten since Lahore was built!"

"May your children prosper!" Labh Singh said, raising his hands in blessing. "May Wahe Guru make you a rich man!"

The momentary bitterness in the atmosphere melted away.

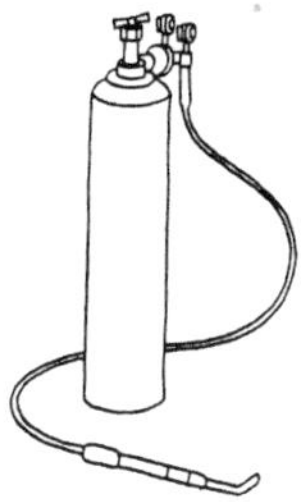

7

SATURDAY.

Karamchand and Guranditta finished their first task at nine p.m. sharp. They had found the underground cable to the police station, dug it up, cut the wire, and reburied it. Now they loaded the tent and equipment into the van—the side of which had been painted with the words TELEPHONE DEPARTMENT, AMRITSAR—and climbed in.

Labh Singh sat in the driver's seat of the van. He looked towards a black Fiat standing about fifty feet away. He turned on the van's headlights and dipped them. Immediately, the Fiat's engine growled to life.

Mayaram was behind the wheel of the Fiat, with Vimal next to him.

Mayaram looked at his watch. He drove the car a short distance and then turned to the right. He wanted to approach the side door of the transport company building from around the back.

Labh Singh put the van in gear and followed him.

Mayaram parked the car in an empty space on the back road. He and Vimal got out. Labh Singh brought the van to a halt near them, and they climbed in.

Labh Singh drove into the alley towards the side entrance.

The alley was deserted.

He stopped the van directly in front of the door.

Mayaram leaped out and reached the door with noiseless steps.

With the keys he'd made in advance, it took about ten seconds to open both the locks. One after another, Guranditta, Karamchand, and Vimal got out of the van. Labh Singh drove the van ahead.

The four went through the door, silent as ghosts. Mayaram left the two keys in the locks. He closed the door from the inside and walked along a passage. There was another door at the other end. This one, too, opened out into the alley, but it was closed from the inside. Mayaram removed the bolt and the iron bar securing the door.

By then, Labh Singh had parked the van and walked back into the alley. He reached the door with the keys in it. He locked both locks from the outside and was at the next door in a few long, silent strides. The others had, with great difficulty, convinced him to wear canvas shoes instead of his usual leather jootis, but they hadn't been able to persuade him to change his tehmad. There was no question of wearing trousers; he wouldn't even agree to a close-fitting pajama.

Once Labh Singh was through the second door, he closed it and threw the bolt.

The five men were inside the transport company building. It had been less than two minutes.

They climbed up the stairs. There was a lift in the building, but the electricity had been shut off when the godown closed.

Mayaram was at the front, since he knew the way. Guranditta and Karamchand followed him, and Labh Singh and Vimal were together at the rear.

Suddenly Labh Singh belched. The odour of whiskey reached Vimal's nostrils.

"Hey Papaji," Vimal said softly, reproachfully. "Didn't we ask you to—"

"Oye, that's nothing, puttar," Labh Singh said, unfazed. "That's just the smell from yesterday. I haven't touched it today."

Labh Singh was lying; Vimal was sure of it. He might not be drunk, but he'd had a peg today for sure.

Once when he stumbled into Vimal in the darkness, Vimal thought he felt a bottle hidden inside the tehmad.

They reached the fourth floor.

Guranditta pulled out a small torch and began to search through the countless packages for the shipment he'd booked for N. Subramanian, Madras. The boxes were quickly found and dragged into a pile in the middle of the hall. Guranditta set to work on the boxes with mechanical swiftness. It took barely ten minutes for all the equipment to be unpacked.

Guranditta and Labh Singh started fitting together the sections of the aluminium ladder. Karamchand looked over the wireless sets to make sure they hadn't been damaged in the packing and unpacking. Mayaram and Vimal carried the gas cylinders and the remaining equipment to the window facing Mehta House.

By a quarter to ten, the ladder was ready. The hall was large, but not big enough to hold a sixty-foot ladder, so they'd opened a door on the far side of the hall to let some of the ladder stick out that way.

Mayaram had memorized the schedule of the guards' rounds; they were due to pass by at nine fifty.

He cautiously opened the window and stood hidden behind one of the shutters, watching the street.

The others stood quietly, waiting.

In a few minutes, the sound of heavy boots came from the street. Mayaram looked out carefully. The only source of light was the shaded bulb below. In its glow, he watched four uniformed guards walk by slowly, talking amongst themselves. They turned the corner and vanished.

"Labh Singh," he said, backing away from the window. "Take care of that bulb."

Labh Singh stepped up without a word. He pulled a catapult and a small stone from his kurta pocket.

"Labh Singh is an expert with the catapult," Mayaram whispered close to Vimal's ear. "Even though the bulb is half-hidden by the shade, he won't need to fire twice. Watch."

Vimal said nothing to that, but he thought that there would have been a better chance if Labh Singh were sober. "Won't anyone get suspicious if the bulb goes off like this?" he asked.

"Bulbs crack all the time in winter," Mayaram replied. "And anyway, it isn't their bulb. It doesn't affect their security arrangement."

Vimal fell silent.

Labh Singh took aim. The bulb broke with a tiny cracking sound. Darkness fell upon the street.

Mayaram looked at his watch—it was nine fifty-five. He swiftly hung the wireless set around his neck and hefted a bag.

"Set up the ladder!" he barked.

Labh Singh, Guranditta, and Vimal began pushing the ladder out of the building. Karamchand picked up another bag.

The far end of the ladder came to rest on the roof of Mehta House. Labh Singh gave it a shake to make sure it was firmly set, then gestured to Mayaram. Mayaram clambered onto the windowsill. He grasped a rung with his hands, adjusted his feet on another rung further back, and began to walk across on all fours, like an animal. The ladder trembled underneath him, but he knew it would bear his weight.

He reached the sloping roof of the bank building.

Once he was off the ladder, Karamchand followed. In a few moments, he joined Mayaram on the bank roof.

The other three pulled the ladder back in and closed the shutters, leaving a narrow gap to look through.

Now the guards arrived again, on their scheduled ten thirteen round.

Mayaram and Karamchand watched them with bated breath. They showed no surprise at finding darkness in the street. Perhaps it was nothing out of the ordinary for them. One guard turned on a torch and lit the way for himself and his comrades. They walked around the corner. The street was empty again.

"Are they humans or machines?" Mayaram muttered to himself. "Not even a second off their schedule!"

"This skirting's not very wide, Ustadji," Karamchand complained.

Mayaram pulled a long nylon rope from his bag. He tied a loop at one end. Karamchand took out a set of pulleys, clamps, and a wire cutter.

The two of them walked along the narrow ledge to the corner. There they clamped the pulleys onto the skirting and ran the rope through the setup. The skirting was made of R.C.C.—strong enough. They had checked the rope and the pulleys beforehand.

They waited.

At ten thirty-seven, the guards went by again. It would be another fifty-three minutes before they came back. There was just enough time.

Karamchand put a foot into the loop at the end of the rope and swung himself off the edge.

Mayaram began to let out the rope. It went down, carrying Karamchand with it. Mayaram had already marked a twenty-five-foot length on the rope, and when he reached it, he stopped. Now his job was to not let the rope slip. He grasped it firmly.

Karamchand found the alarm wire coming out of the conduit pipe. He took the wire cutter from his pocket and snipped it, holding on to the rope with his other hand. The wire was live—the two cut ends touched briefly and sparked—but the cutter had insulated handles, so Karamchand was safe. He tugged at the rope.

Mayaram began pulling him up. By the time Karamchand reached the skirting, they were both out of breath.

One alarm had been successfully taken care of.

Without pausing to catch their breath, they began dismantling the pulleys with a spanner and screwdriver.

Then they moved to the next corner. It was delicate work and required patience, but they were in a hurry—the more time they spent here, the less time they would have to open the safe.

By a quarter past eleven, they were done with the alarms on all four corners, and were standing on the skirting facing the transport company office.

There were still fifteen minutes left before the next patrol.

They fitted the pulleys onto the skirting directly opposite the transport company window. This time, Karamchand did not need to descend very far. There was a window just eight feet below the roof. The glass panes of the window were bolted from the inside. Since there were alarms in the building, the panes weren't considered a weak spot—besides, they were forty-seven feet from the ground.

Karamchand used a diamond glass cutter to make a circle in the windowpane. It made a scratching sound, but he felt sure that no one would hear it. He tapped the centre of the circle and the glass fell away. He put a hand through the hole. Just before he touched the bolt, he paused. His entire body was tensed. What if there was another alarm they didn't know about?

He touched the bolt. Nothing happened. Taking a deep breath, he pulled it; it slid out easily. He opened the window and climbed in. Then he tugged lightly on the rope.

Mayaram pulled it in, and then swiftly began dismantling the pulley set and stuffing it into the tool bag. He put on the headphones of the wireless set, and switched it on.

"Hello," Vimal's voice came from the other side.

"Ladder." Mayaram said just the one word and pulled off the headphones, hanging them around his neck.

He looked at his watch. They only had four more minutes before the patrol came back. The window opened and the ladder was once more extended out to the roof of the bank. Mayaram set the end down securely and climbed with monkey-like agility back across to the transport company.

They pulled the ladder back in as fast as they could.

The guards stepped into the street as the last two rungs of the ladder were disappearing from view. Then the ladder was in, and the windows quickly closed.

This patrol, too, turned the corner. Now the gang had some time before the next round—an hour and twenty-three minutes.

Mayaram was happy. So far, everything was going like clockwork. They had broken into the unbreakable Mehta House. One of the gang was already inside the bank.

The window was opened again and the ladder was extended. This time, it was aimed not at the roof, but at the open window where Karamchand was waiting. Karamchand used a piece of wire to tie a rung of the ladder to the window frame so that it would not slip.

Mayaram started across the ladder first, carrying a gas cylinder; then came Vimal, then Guranditta, as Labh Singh held the ladder from the other end. After two more trips, the three of them had carried all the equipment across. They moved so quickly and quietly that it seemed like they had rehearsed it many times before. To Vimal, everyone seemed to be doing their jobs efficiently and capably—even Labh Singh.

Finally, Karamchand went back and Labh Singh came into the bank. He hadn't slung his tehmad around his neck as promised, but he had doubled it and tucked it in at the waist, so it was above his knees.

Karamchand pulled the ladder back into the transport company building and closed the window. Mayaram closed the window of the bank.

"We need to get all this equipment to the ground floor hall," he said.

Everyone nodded, and they picked up as much as they could carry.

In just one trip, all of the equipment was in the lit hall on the ground floor. The bright light of the hall had a sobering effect—everyone felt more exposed. Guranditta, especially, was looking nervous.

Mayaram looked at his watch. It was nearly twelve.

They still had plenty of time before the next patrol. That meant that no one would be looking through the peephole in the front door in the near future. But something in Mayaram's brain wanted more reassurance. What if some guard in the compound decided to take a random look and ruined everything?

Then he remembered the wireless set around his neck. He put on the headphones, pressed a button, turned the handle to charge it, and called to Karamchand. "Can you see the front door of the bank from where you are?"

"No," Karamchand's voice crackled. "I can see the compound but not the door."

"Find a window from which you can see the door. Go down a floor if you have to. Call me when you're there."

"Okay."

Mayaram fell silent. He kept the wireless set running.

In a short while, Karamchand's voice came through. "Ustadji, I can see the front door now."

"Any guards close to it?"

"No, but there are two in the compound."

"Okay. We're moving to the basement. If any of them moves towards the door, let us know."

"All right."

Mayaram gestured to the rest. Guranditta and Vimal each picked up a cylinder, Labh Singh picked up two, and they moved forward stealthily. Crossing the hall, they reached the basement staircase and went down single file.

Two minutes later, they reappeared empty-handed, Guranditta in the lead. Mayaram motioned to them to stay close.

Two more rounds carrying equipment, and then everything was downstairs. The other three remained there, and Mayaram came back up to the hall. He turned on the wireless and asked, "Karamchand, what's the status outside?"

"All fine, Ustadji," Karamchand's voice said.

"I'm going down. Stay alert. If you see anything odd, call me at once."

"Yes."

He took off the headphones, turned off the wireless, and quickly walked downstairs again. The hair on the back of his neck prickled. He couldn't shake the feeling that any moment now, a gunshot would ring out and he would collapse like a felled tree.

When he reached the basement, he felt a little reassured. The others were waiting for him in the dark.

Mayaram turned on his torch and looked for the switchboard. He flipped a couple of switches. The basement flooded with light. In an alcove at the other end of the long room, the gigantic door to the vault loomed.

"God!" Guranditta exclaimed, mesmerized.

The door was six feet high and four feet wide, and seemed a mile thick.

Mayaram noticed two exhaust fans above the alcove. Instead of an open space beyond them, there was a duct leading off somewhere. He hesitated for a moment, then found the switches for the fans. They began to turn silently. They were so powerful that the men's hair fluttered and they felt the cold. The three of them began to set up the gas cylinders and the blowtorch.

Mayaram took out a piece of chalk and a nail, and pulled a foot ruler from one of the bags. He measured some distances on the vault door, then drew a rough circle about two feet wide below the dial. Within this, he scratched out a smaller circle, and finally a small cross in the centre. This was the spot where the door was to be melted.

By now the blowtorch was ready.

Mayaram opened two buttons of his shirt and wrapped a towel around his neck. He put on gloves and welder's goggles. Guranditta handed him the lit torch. Mayaram took it, then paused for a moment. "No, this won't work. Get a chair."

There were three or four chairs by the staircase. Vimal brought one over. Mayaram sat on it. He rested his elbows on his knees and then, holding the flame absolutely steady, aimed it at the cross on the door. The aluminium paint burned away instantly with a *whoosh*, smoke filled the air, and then the steel began to melt. Sparks flew around the flame. In just five minutes, it was so hot near the vault that sweat began to shine on everyone's faces. Labh Singh, Guranditta, and Vimal drew back to the other side of the room.

The sweat began to flow into Mayaram's eyes. He was having trouble keeping them open. He gritted his teeth, making an effort to hold the torch steady. The melted steel flowed like wax down the door. There was nothing complicated about it, except that the door seemed to be melting too slowly. The job needed time. With enough gas and enough patience, any door, no matter how thick, could be bored through. But would his estimate prove correct? Mayaram worried over the question. Would five hours be enough time?

Finally, when he could no longer keep the flame steady, he said, "Labh Singh, take over."

"Give it to Guranditta now, Ustadji," Labh Singh said, flustered. "I need to take a piss."

"The bitch is supposed to be on a hunt, and it wants to go and shit," Mayaram said, irritated. "Don't go upstairs, Labh Singh. Do it somewhere around here."

"Okay," Labh Singh said, and turned away.

Guranditta set goggles over his eyes, took the torch from Mayaram, and sat down in his place.

Mayaram walked away, drenched in sweat. He threw down his goggles and began to wipe himself off with his towel.

"Take the coat off, Ustadji," Vimal suggested.

"That's all right," Mayaram said. "Won't make much difference, anyhow."

Vimal fell silent. He lit a cigarette.

"Give me one," Mayaram said.

Vimal handed him the packet and the matches. A thought came to him. He walked towards the stairs quietly. Mayaram paid no attention.

As he reached the stairs, Vimal saw that Labh Singh was pissing in a corner, his back to him. One hand was occupied with his business, while the other held a half-bottle of whiskey to his mouth.

Vimal coughed quietly.

Labh Singh, startled, looked back. He quickly dropped his tehmad, and laughed guiltily.

"Want some matar-paneer with that?" Vimal asked him.

Labh Singh looked even guiltier.

Vimal turned around. Labh Singh threw the empty bottle under the stairs and followed him.

Vimal walked back towards the vault. There were four buckets next to the fire extinguishers, filled with sand and water. Mayaram had set one of these down on the floor, and was dipping his head into it. He took out his head and splashed water down his open shirt. His face looked red and dried out. He put a lump of salt into his mouth, poured some glucose from a packet in after it, and then took a few gulps of coffee from a flask.

Vimal looked at his watch. Mayaram had worked the torch for only twenty minutes. After that short stint, he looked like he'd crawled for hours through a burning desert.

Vimal saw that Labh Singh, though still ten feet away from the vault, was already drenched in sweat. He was fatter than Mayaram, and then there was the heat from the whiskey… He hadn't even touched the torch, and already he looked as bad as Mayaram. Only his breathing was still normal.

"Shall I try next?" Vimal said, after a while.

"No," Mayaram said, "You won't be able to do this. Chal oye, Labh Singh!"

Labh Singh went up to Guranditta.

"You should have some experience with welding for this," Mayaram told Vimal. "The flame needs to be held very steady on one spot."

"That's funny," Vimal said. "Why am I even here, then? If all you needed was a coolie to carry your stuff—"

"Don't act stupid. You know perfectly well why you're here. Do you think I'd let you out of my sight at this stage? You could've gotten all of us nabbed. If the cops got to know about us, all this effort would've been for nothing."

"You're too suspicious," Vimal said, annoyed.

"Too bad, if that's what you think. I think it would be safest if, at least for tonight, I keep you with me."

Vimal said nothing.

Labh Singh sat down in Guranditta's place.

Guranditta got up, gasping for breath, and immediately tore off his clothes. Leaving only his underwear on, he sat down on the floor and began to towel himself off.

"Hell!" he muttered. "What heat! Whether or not that door melts, it's hot enough to melt a man!"

"Three thousand degrees is no joke." Mayaram handed him the box of glucose and a lump of salt.

"Hell, absolute hell!" Guranditta said again.

"Ustadji, the gas is finished," Labh Singh cut in.

Mayaram saw that the flame from the torch was dying down. He signalled to Vimal, who rolled another cylinder over. Mayaram replaced the empty cylinder with the new one. The flame rose up again.

Labh Singh began to focus it on the molten door.

Mayaram looked at him for a few seconds, then hissed, "Labh Singh, you idiot, steady your hand!"

"Not to worry, Ustadji!" Labh Singh said with calm confidence.

"Why shouldn't I worry?" Mayaram said. "Your hand's going all over the place!"

"It only shook a little; it's all right now."

Labh Singh's hand really did steady. But after a couple of minutes, it wandered again.

"Oye, Sikhe!" Mayaram yelled threateningly.

Labh Singh let out a strange noise. The flame steadied, moved, steadied again, then went on moving.

Mayaram gritted his teeth. He looked at Guranditta helplessly.

"He's drunk," Vimal said.

"How do you know?" Mayaram whirled on him.

"He'd already had some when he started from home, and he was drinking again just now. When he pretended to be pissing."

"Why didn't you tell me?"

"What for? It's only young cockerels like me who lose control when they drink. *He* just gets smarter and more alert."

Mayaram looked at Labh Singh again. Hopelessness replaced the rage on his face. It was as if he could see all his plans shattering to bits.

"Wait and see," Vimal said. "He'll fall off the ladder when we're going back."

"Shut up," said Mayaram, angrily. He put on the gloves and goggles and walked up to Labh Singh. He snatched the torch from him.

"What happened?" Labh Singh said, startled.

"Bastard! May you get shot! May you get bitten by a snake!" Mayaram barked at him. "Get up!"

Labh Singh stood up. Mayaram pushed him away and sat down.

The flame, once again steady, focused on the door.

Mayaram stayed in the chair for half an hour, after which Guranditta took his place. Mayaram was so weak when he got up that he could barely stand. He got away from the chair and then lay down flat on the floor.

"Oxygen!" Guranditta said to Vimal.

Vimal brought over the oxygen cylinder. He took off Mayaram's goggles and fitted the gas mask over his mouth. Mayaram took several deep breaths, and a bit of life came back into him. He pushed the gas mask away.

Labh Singh sat with his back to the wall, blinking owlishly, looking around aimlessly.

Vimal handed Mayaram the coffee and glucose.

Five minutes later, Mayaram had recovered.

"Take off the coat, Ustadji," Vimal said.

"It's all right," Mayaram said, "It won't make any—"

"Ustadji," Vimal said softly, "If you think I haven't already noticed the gun in your shoulder holster, then you're kidding yourself."

Mayaram looked at him, eyes widening.

"Didn't you say something about not bringing any firearms?"

"I hadn't planned to. This isn't going to be any use, anyway," Mayaram said. "But God knows what got into me this evening. I took it without even realizing what I was doing."

Vimal said nothing.

Mayaram pulled off his clothes, keeping the gun out of sight. "We're ten inches deep so far," he said.

"Hmm."

"Labh Singh, that idiot, has bungled things up. It's hotter than I expected. Look at the state I was in! It's going to be impossible for just the two of us to do this."

"Try me," Vimal said. "It doesn't seem as difficult as you're making it out to be."

Mayaram looked at Labh Singh doubtfully. "How much did he drink?" he asked.

"He drank a half-bottle measure before my eyes," Vimal said. "God only knows how much he drank at home."

"In that case, it's amazing that he's even conscious. He ought to have been snoring by now."

Just then, the wireless set beeped.

Mayaram put on the headphones, turned on the set, and said, "Karamchand!"

"Yes," the voice came through. "What's going on, Ustadji?"

"All fine," Mayaram said, "What about you?"

"All fine."

"Good." He took off the headphones.

When Guranditta got up, he was even worse off than Mayaram. By then the second gas cylinder was empty, too. Mayaram connected the new cylinder and said to Vimal, "All right, then. Have a go."

Vimal put on the gloves and goggles, and sat down.

Mayaram handed him the torch. "Keep your elbows firm on your knees and focus the flame right here. That's all you need to do."

Vimal nodded.

"In a couple of minutes, you'll begin to feel the heat. One way to cope with it is to think of something else. Think of the wealth that we're going to get. Think of the women you've partied with. Think of all the good times..."

Or dream of the wealth that I've lost, Vimal thought. *Think of all the women I never paid attention to while I was busy being faithful to the wife who betrayed me. Think of all the hard times I went through—that I'm still going through—all because of her.*

If all it took to escape the heat was to think of something else, then Surjeet Kaur would give him enough to brood over.

"Good!" Mayaram was saying, somewhere, "Well done!"

Vimal was lost in thought. *What was Surjeet doing these days? Was she still in Allahabad, enjoying her life with that bastard Gyan Prakash Dogra? To hell with her! She can do what she wants. She isn't my wife any more. Now I'm...*

"Get up."

His reverie broke. Mayaram was patting his shoulder. He handed the torch to him and stood up. He realized that his body was as hot as an ember. Red stars danced in front of his eyes, and his brain felt like it was floating away. He lay down and began to take deep breaths.

Labh Singh had fallen asleep where he sat, and now the snores had started.

"Put some salt in your mouth," Guranditta said.

Vimal did as he was told. Then he ate some glucose and swallowed some coffee. He began to feel better. He didn't use the oxygen mask.

By now the whole basement was quite hot, but it was bearable away from the vault. There was a little breeze blowing near the stairs, and Vimal went towards it.

Suddenly Mayaram gave a little shout. Vimal, startled, ran back.

He saw that Mayaram's sweat-drenched, reddened face was alight with jubilation.

"We've done it!" he declared.

"What happened? Is the door open?" Vimal asked him.

"The hole's gone right through the door," Guranditta said.

"What? Just a hole?"

"Yes, but that was the hard part. That was the biggest challenge. Enlarging the hole will be easy."

"Oh."

Guranditta picked up the torch.

Mayaram seemed to have regained his enthusiasm. His spirits had picked up now that he could see some results. He seemed especially happy with Vimal, because his help had gotten them out of a bad situation.

By four thirty in the morning, the unbreakable, two and a half foot thick door had a window in it, two feet high and two and a half feet wide. The opening was enough for a thin man to go through easily.

In enlarging the opening, they had nearly finished the last gas cylinder. If the hole had been too small, there was neither enough gas nor enough time to do anything about it.

But they weren't done yet. A huge problem still stared them in the face.

The door glowed like lava.

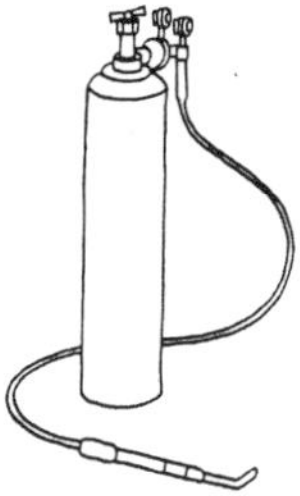

8

"LABH SINGH!" MAYARAM GROWLED, kicking him awake. "Get up, you lout!"

Labh Singh stood up and rubbed his eyes. He looked around, blinking, as if he didn't understand where he was. Then he noticed the door of the vault. A wave of happiness crossed his face, and he burst out, "Wahe Guru sacche Paatshah!" He leapt towards the door.

Mayaram grabbed his arm and pulled him back. "Idiot, you'll get roasted like a kebab!"

Labh Singh stopped, blinking foolishly.

Mayaram picked up the half-filled bucket on the floor and tossed the water at the door. There was a loud hissing, and the entire room filled with steam.

"Oh!" Labh Singh cried out.

"Turn on this fire extinguisher and spray it at the door," Mayaram said. "We'll rest for a while."

Labh Singh nodded and picked up the extinguisher. He turned it over, hit its cap on the floor, and aimed the hose. Foam began to spray onto the door. The room echoed with hisses. Mayaram, Guranditta, and Vimal lay down on the floor. They closed their eyes and tried to breathe deeply.

Labh Singh continued working to cool down the door.

When their eyes opened, white foam had covered the door and was dripping down to the floor.

Mayaram looked at his watch. It was a quarter past five.

He approached the door for a closer look. It no longer glowed, but it was still hot enough to sear flesh.

Mayaram gestured to Vimal. Vimal picked up another fire extinguisher and joined Labh Singh.

Mayaram and Guranditta began clearing every surface they'd touched to remove fingerprints—the empty gas cylinders, the torch, the thermos, the glucose box, the buckets, the floor, the walls, the switches, everything. Once done, they put on close-fitting rubber gloves. They took the extinguishers from Vimal and Labh Singh and wiped them down, too. Vimal and Labh Singh put on gloves as well.

At a quarter to six, the door still wasn't completely cooled down, but they thought they could get through it—provided they moved swiftly and carefully.

They put aside the extinguishers and poured sand over the hot bottom rim of the hole. Then they set soaking-wet gunny bags around the edges.

Mayaram dressed again, and was the first to put his head in through the opening. Labh Singh quickly pushed him in, and he fell into the vault.

Guranditta and Vimal followed him.

Labh Singh stayed outside—he was too fat to get in through the hole. He handed Mayaram four large canvas bags.

Mayaram found a light switch inside the vault and turned it on.

The vault was as big as a room. Steel trays packed with bundles of notes lined all the walls. Vimal held a bag open, and Mayaram and Guranditta began picking up the trays and pouring the notes into the bag.

"Guranditta," Mayaram said, "don't take these fifties."

"Why?"

"These are brand-new notes. They'll get noticed even if there aren't any records of their numbers—could get us caught."

"Oh. Right."

"They'll take up too much space, anyway," Mayaram added.

When the first bag was full, Vimal handed it to Labh Singh, who tied it closed with a rope. Then the second. Then the third. They never got to the fourth.

"Stop," Mayaram said. "It's six o'clock. No time left. If we get too greedy, we'll lose whatever we have."

They began to climb out of the vault.

Vimal was last to go.

Just before he stepped out, he paused. Hesitating a little, he picked up two bundles of fifty-rupee notes from a tray. He stuffed the notes into an inner pocket of his coat and climbed out.

"How much do you think it is?" Labh Singh was saying, a tremor in his voice.

"Not less than sixty or sixty-five lakhs!" Mayaram said. "They're all hundreds."

"Balle!"

Mayaram switched on the wireless set. The coast would be clear—the six o'clock patrol would have just passed by—but Mayaram wanted to be sure.

"Ustadji," Karamchand's impatient voice came through. "What happened?"

"Victory! We're coming back. Is the coast clear?"

"Yes. The guards just passed by."

"Get to the window with the ladder."

"Right."

Mayaram switched off the wireless.

Mayaram, Guranditta, and Vimal had been fighting the vault door for five and a half hours, and the three of them felt like they were falling apart. Mayaram, perhaps, was caught up in the ecstasy of victory, and he was anyway used to hard labour. Vimal had spent comparatively less time behind the torch. But Guranditta was the worst off of them all. He had carried his bag of money barely two steps when he stumbled, and his knees began to buckle. The result was that Labh Singh had to carry his bag, too. Vimal carried the third bag. Mayaram led the way, carrying only the wireless set. Guranditta followed him, with one hand on his shoulder for support. His legs still wobbled, but somehow they managed to carry him as he went on.

They climbed up the stairs and flashed past the hall.

The next patrol—the last one—was at six fifty-three.

They began to climb the second flight of stairs.

"Guranditta!" Mayaram said, "Careful!"

"Unhhh…" Guranditta groaned. His voice sounded like it was coming from the bottom of a well.

They reached the window they'd entered by. Mayaram looked out. It was still dark, and the street was deserted.

He switched on the wireless. As soon as Karamchand responded, he said "Ladder."

The window across the alley opened and the ladder came out, moving slowly towards them.

Guranditta sat down on the floor, his back to the wall.

"Guranditta!" Mayaram said roughly. "Get up! Just five minutes more!"

"Unhhh..."

"We need to take care of him," Mayaram said to Vimal. "Don't let him sleep."

Vimal nodded, then looked towards Labh Singh. Was he still drunk, or had it worn off? He didn't look very alert. But Vimal couldn't decide.

The ladder reached their window.

Mayaram grasped the ladder, let a couple of rungs come into the room. Then he tied the ladder to the window with a rope. For the last time, he called up Karamchand on the wireless to tell him they were coming, and then he dropped the set where he stood.

Vimal picked up a bag and climbed onto the ladder. It was a large bag—a gunny sack really—and though it held only paper, it was quite heavy. He began to creep slowly across the ladder, looking only at where his next step would be. He couldn't muster the courage to look down.

He reached the other end safely.

Karamchand greeted him enthusiastically. He caressed the bag of money like a new father seeing his baby for the first time.

Then Labh Singh got onto the ladder, carrying a bag.

Vimal had his heart in his mouth until Labh Singh was across safely. He kept expecting something to go wrong. He relaxed only when Labh Singh was done.

Then Guranditta climbed on, empty-handed. He began to crawl across slowly. By now he realized the difficulty of his task. He was moving very carefully, crouched like an animal.

He reached the halfway point. Then, suddenly, he was not on the ladder.

Something thudded onto the street below, and Vimal realized what had happened.

He stood dumbstruck. For a second, he couldn't figure out what to do. Karamchand and Labh Singh were frozen, too. Whether it was because the ladder had wobbled, or he'd lost his grip on a rung, or lost his footing—whatever had happened, Guranditta had fallen off the ladder and plunged fifty feet.

Vimal saw Mayaram, and felt goosebumps rise on the back of his neck. Mayaram was on the ladder, bag in hand. But he wasn't crawling. He stood straight up on the rungs and *ran*, as if he was running on a footpath instead of a ladder fifty feet above the ground. In the dark, he could only guess where the rungs were. It looked as if he was running on air.

In an instant, he was by their side.

"Run! Get down!" he bellowed.

Their trance was broken. They began to run, pushing, shoving each other.

Mayaram ran as if he had wings. He felt as if he'd piloted his ship home through the storm, but now he was sinking at the shore. He reached the ground floor before anyone else, opened the bolt, and pushed the door open. He threw the bag down into the alley and shouted, "Labh Singh, get the car!"

Labh Singh threw his bag down and sprinted down the alley. In spite of his weight, he was moving very quickly, tehmad held above his knees.

Mayaram ran in the opposite direction.

Vimal hesitated a moment, then, leaving his bag, followed Mayaram.

Karamchand stood foolishly, rooted to the spot. At his feet lay unclaimed the enormous wealth he'd always dreamed of.

Mayaram turned the corner and reached the street where Guranditta lay. He paused. No one seemed to have heard the sound of the fall. Guranditta hadn't uttered a word. The thud of his body hitting the ground had probably not reached the guards.

Mayaram realized that Vimal was following him. He waited for him to catch up, and the two ran towards Guranditta's inert body. Without bothering to check whether he was alive, they each grabbed one arm and began to haul him off like a dead dog. Guranditta's heels dragged along roughly on the road behind them.

They halted only when they had turned the corner.

After a pause, they picked him up again. This time, Vimal picked up both arms, and Mayaram the legs. Guranditta's body scrunched into an impossible position between them. It felt as if his spine had come undone and many other bones, too, were broken. Vimal felt nauseous. He bit his lip and looked away as he moved.

All was quiet. The plan had only just been salvaged.

When they reached the next lane, Labh Singh brought the car over. Vimal and Mayaram dumped the body into the back seat.

They both piled into the front seat next to Labh Singh. The car reversed back to the transport company entrance, and they all got out.

Labh Singh swiftly opened the boot of the car.

The three bags went in. He closed the boot and locked it, and came back to the driver's seat. The other three fit somehow into the front seat. Mayaram saw that Karamchand still had the wireless set around his neck.

"Karamchand!" he said, "What are you going to do with that wireless now, pickle it?"

Karamchand fumbled with the set and finally threw it out the window of the moving car.

Mayaram struggled to turn around. He managed to reach Guranditta, checked his pulse and then his heart.

"Finished!" he said.

A heavy silence fell over the car.

Labh Singh turned to the right.

Dawn was breaking. The sky was getting brighter.

They had left the fifty-foot ladder bridging the two buildings. Mayaram had wanted to remove it, but now there was no time, and with what they had in the back seat, they had to get away as soon as possible. The ladder would give them away very quickly.

Labh Singh stopped the car as they drew up alongside the van. Mayaram got out, and Vimal followed.

"You stay in the car," Mayaram said.

"No," Vimal said determinedly, "I can't sit close to Guranditta. Just thinking about him makes me want to throw up."

"All right then. Come along."

They got into the van, Mayaram driving.

The car began to move. The van followed it.

The impossible had been done. The "impregnable" bank had been looted. Mayaram had pulled it off.

It was now light, but on that winter morning, the roads were still lonely. Once in a while they passed a bus, or a rickshaw, or a cyclist. They saw one or two milkmen and newspaper boys delivering their goods.

"We have to get rid of Guranditta's body," Mayaram said suddenly. "Otherwise we'll all get caught."

"What do we do?" Vimal asked him.

"We'll stage an accident. We'll make it look like he crashed his car."

"Where do we do it?"

Mayaram continued driving for a while, looking thoughtfully at the car ahead of him. They were heading towards Putli Ghar.

Suddenly Mayaram sped up the van, and pulled alongside the car. He honked the horn until Labh Singh looked at him. Labh Singh stopped the car, and Mayaram stopped next to him.

"What?" Labh Singh said, sticking his head out.

"Don't stop at Putli Ghar," Mayaram said. "Keep going—onto the Attari road."

"Why?"

"We have to take care of Guranditta."

Mayaram drove ahead of the car, leading the way.

"Shouldn't we take care of the loot first?" Vimal asked.

"Where do we put it?" Mayaram said. "We were going to put it in Guranditta's workshop. He's gone now, so how can we leave it there?"

Vimal said nothing.

"Let's just get rid of Guranditta, then split the loot and go our own ways."

"All right."

The van moved out of the city, past Chheharta. Labh Singh kept the car close to the van.

The road was almost empty. They had travelled quite a distance.

"Do you plan to go all the way to Pakistan?" Vimal asked, finally.

"No. Just five minutes more," Mayaram said. "We're almost there. We'll finish it off way before Attari."

A little later, Mayaram stopped the van. Labh Singh pulled up behind him. All of them got out.

The sun was still not visible, but daylight had spread through the sky. A pleasant cool breeze blew.

Vimal saw that where they'd stopped, the road was elevated, and it took a sharp turn just ahead. There were wooden railings along both sides of the road, and about twenty feet beyond, the ground fell away amidst dense foliage.

"This spot will be fine," Mayaram said. "We'll put Guranditta in the driver's seat of the car and push it down here. People will think that he didn't slow down at the turn, and the car broke through the railings and went down."

Labh Singh got into the car and drove it to the front of the van. They moved the bags of money from the car boot to the van.

The next part was taken care of by Labh Singh and Mayaram, since neither Vimal nor Karamchand could bear to look at the body, let alone touch it. They took Guranditta out of the back seat and sat him in the driver's seat. Labh Singh stuck his hands on the steering wheel. Since his back was broken, he wouldn't stay upright.

Labh Singh left the keys in the ignition.

The car was pointing towards the railings.

Mayaram got into the van. He started it, and slowly nudged it into the car's rear bumper. He pressed on the accelerator gently. The car moved forward, pushed from behind. It paused for a second, held back by the railing. Mayaram carefully pressed the pedal, afraid that the van would follow the car down if he went too far.

Finally the wooden railing splintered and broke away to both sides. The car went down.

Mayaram stomped on the brake. The van's wheels stopped just short of the sharply sloping earth.

The car did a somersault and crashed into the narrow valley.

Mayaram reversed the van, turned off the ignition, and jumped out. Thankfully, during all this, no one had driven by. He went up to the railing and looked down.

Labh Singh had deliberately left the driver's side door open. When the car had started its fall, Guranditta's body had been thrown out. Now the car was on its side in a ditch and the body was about three feet away, facedown in some shrubs.

The break in the railing, too, looked quite natural.

The accident seemed entirely believable. The driver had been careless, failed to slow down in time or steer the car around. It had gone out of control, broken through the railing, and fallen.

A bus passed by, but it neither slowed down nor stopped. No one seemed to have noticed the broken railing.

"You stay here," Mayaram said. "I'll turn the van around."

Everyone nodded in agreement.

He moved towards the van. A sudden urge made Vimal follow him.

Mayaram looked at him strangely, but said nothing.

Vimal had been growing increasingly suspicious that Mayaram intended to get away with all of the loot, and this was the perfect chance. The rest of them would be left behind on the road, and Mayaram would get away in the van. Vimal made sure to climb in before him.

Mayaram came around and got into the driver's seat. He drove the van a short distance forward, turned it around, and brought it back towards Labh Singh and Karamchand.

As the van came closer, instead of slowing down, Mayaram pressed the accelerator. The van leapt forward.

Vimal was thrown back, hitting the seat hard. He turned to look at Mayaram, bewildered. Mayaram was gritting his teeth, and there was a demonic gleam in his eyes.

Suddenly he twisted the steering wheel to the left. Karamchand, or perhaps Labh Singh, screamed. The van took both of them down before they could get clear.

Vimal squeezed his eyes shut.

There was a crash, and the van jumped. Then Vimal was thrown forward, towards the dashboard. He opened his eyes and looked around, terrified. Labh Singh and Karamchand were nowhere to be seen.

Mayaram was pulling at the steering wheel with all his might, trying to get the van back on the road.

Vimal looked behind him. He could see two shapeless piles of flesh on the road. Something screamed inside him.

"This...this..." he stammered, terrified. "What did you do?"

"Shut up!" Mayaram growled.

"But...but..."

"Idiot! Start thinking of a half-share now, instead of one-fifth."

"But...that Labh Singh...he was your friend...your childhood friend!"

"And I killed him." Mayaram laughed. "Though he was my dearest friend. And you? You're nothing to me."

"What do you mean?"

Mayaram took one hand off the steering wheel and pointed his gun at Vimal's head.

Vimal's mouth felt dry. So Mayaram had planned this from the beginning! That was why he'd stopped everyone else from carrying a gun and brought one himself!

But could he shoot Vimal in the moving van?

They were approaching a curve. Mayaram shifted gears and put his foot on the brake to slow down.

Vimal swung his leg out and stamped his foot down on Mayaram's as hard as he could. The van's tyres squealed. Mayaram fell forward onto the steering wheel.

"You son of a—" he yelled.

The hand holding the gun hit the dashboard, but Mayaram's finger was stuck in the trigger, so the gun didn't fall. The van swerved wildly. Vimal opened the door on his side and jumped out. He fell onto the road, on his shoulder. A wave of pain shot through his body, but the van had slowed down considerably by then, so he wasn't too badly hurt. He continued to roll along the road and fell off into a ditch. There were bushes ahead of him. He crawled swiftly into them.

By now Mayaram had the van under control. He stopped it some distance ahead, then came walking back. He'd hidden the hand with the gun in his pocket. He stopped at the spot where Vimal had jumped out, and began to look around desperately.

Vimal had crawled further into the cover of the vegetation.

"Vimal!" Mayaram called out suddenly.

Vimal stopped. The bushes might stir when he moved, which would give Mayaram a target.

But now the sun was out and traffic had picked up. Could Mayaram use his gun in the open like this? Vimal picked up a stone and threw it.

A shot rang out.

Vimal thought it was best to stay where he was. Mayaram could not leave the lakhs of rupees unguarded in the van while he searched every inch of earth for him.

Time went by; Vimal stayed still, nerves taut.

Then he heard the van starting up.

Still, he did not get up. This might be another trick—if he raised his head, Mayaram might fire at him.

He heard the van moving away.

By the time Vimal gathered up the courage to take a look, the van was back in Amritsar.

Overleaf: Raja Pocket Books Advertisement for "The 25th Silver Jubilee novel in Surender Mohan Pathak's 'Vimal' series: *Maut Ke Munh Mein* (In the Jaws of Death)".

सुरेन्द्र मोहन पाठक
विमल
सीरीज
का
वां सिल्वर ज़ुबली

पंडती

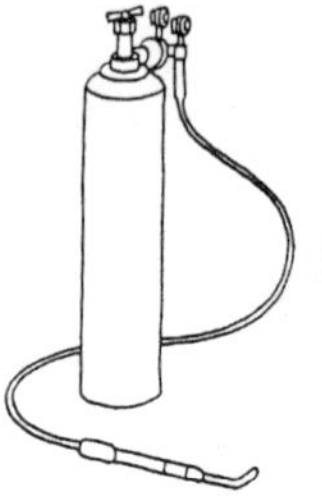

9

VIMAL WOKE UP AT EIGHT in the evening.

He saw there was darkness in the room and outside, and pushed himself off the bed. He had been asleep for twelve or thirteen hours.

It was Sunday, and he was not usually required at his job on Sundays. That was why he hadn't been awakened yet.

He went down to the bungalow and found out that the Lala had taken his wife to the club. He went to see if there was anything to eat in the kitchen.

Both the servants were there. They were discussing the current news, but they hadn't mentioned the heist. Either the robbery hadn't been discovered yet, or the servants hadn't heard of it. From the discussion, Vimal also guessed that no one had noticed he hadn't been in his room the previous night.

He came out of the kitchen and walked to the road. He thought for a while, trying to decide on his next step. Then, nodding his head decisively, he started off. He would need a lot of patience and cunning for what was to come.

He talked to rickshaw-walas, tonga-walas, likely-looking people around paan shops and permit rooms, people at tiny eateries, asking whether they had heard of one Mayaram Bawa, a.k.a. Ustadji—or else of Harnam Singh Garewal, the dada.

No one knew. Or at least, no one talked.

But Vimal persisted. This wasn't a task to be finished in a few hours. Amritsar was no small hamlet; the search could take a while. Several people did not flat-out deny knowing Ustadji and Garewal. They wanted to know why he was asking—Vimal evaded the topic.

One man said he knew Harnam Singh Garewal, but not his whereabouts. He didn't even know whether he lived in Amritsar. Vimal thought he was lying. Perhaps, in the man's mind, it was an honour to know Garewal.

Vimal returned to Ajit Nagar. He planned to take his search to another area the next day.

The heist was front-page news in the papers the next morning. On Sunday morning, someone had noticed the ladder bridging the transport company office and the bank. Then he'd seen the open window of the bank.

The guards had panicked.

The vault was checked immediately, and the theft discovered.

According to the paper, the heist had been pulled off with such finesse that none of the security staff had even the tiniest inkling. But for the ladder, no one would have found out until Monday morning, when the bank opened.

The paper called it "the most sensational robbery in the history of Punjab." It ran photos of the breached vault door, the gas cylinders in the basement, the opened window, Mehta House and the building next to it. No fingerprints had been found—except on a half-bottle of whiskey. No one was sure whether the bottle had been left behind by the robbers or by some staff member earlier.

Elsewhere in the paper was a smaller story of the accident at Khasa, and of the two people crushed by some heavy vehicle next to it. There were no clues to the identity of the accident victim or of the two bodies.

The newspaper made no connections between these incidents and the heist.

On Monday, Vimal continued his search for Mayaram and Harnam Singh Garewal.

He found nothing.

On Tuesday, a truck driver drinking in a restaurant next to Chitra Cinema told him that while he himself knew nothing of Garewal, he knew someone who definitely would.

Vimal's hopes rose.

The truck driver told Vimal that there was a restaurant called Rajmahal, on Queen's Road, run by a Kashmiri named Kaul. Kaul was the only way one could contact Garewal—there was no direct route. Kaul would size the person up, then tell Garewal, and if Garewal thought the person was on the level, a meeting would be fixed. What that meant was, if some crook had a plan that he needed Garewal's help with, he would have to spell it out to Kaul first. Then Kaul and Garewal would decide together whether the plan was worth getting into. This arrangement ensured that the wrong type of person—say, an informer or an undercover cop—couldn't get to Garewal.

Vimal found a rickshaw and set off to Queen's Road.

There were some new things about the heist in the newspaper that day. It had been established that the black Fiat that had crashed near Khasa was almost certainly involved in the heist. The tyre treads matched those found near the transport company. It didn't prove anything conclusively, but the detectives who'd arrived from Calcutta and Delhi to investigate were assuming that this had been the getaway car.

Fingerprints had been recovered from the ladder that had been left behind. The prints proved that there were at least five people involved in the heist. The prints had been sent to the Records Department, but there were no matches yet. The prints on the whiskey bottle matched one of the sets on the ladder, which proved that it had belonged to one of the robbers. Investigations were continuing.

The plan had been to clean off the fingerprints from the ladder and everything in the godown as well, but the incident with Guranditta had made them panicky and they'd forgotten.

There was nothing about Labh Singh and Karamchand's bodies in today's paper.

When Vimal had been caught during the bank van robbery in Delhi, his fingerprints had been taken. Copies of the prints from the ladder were to be sent to every state, so at some point it would come out that the notorious criminal Sardar Surender Singh Sohal was involved in this heist, too.

This worried Vimal. It meant he couldn't stay in Amritsar for long. He would have to get as far from the scene of the crime as possible.

He got off the rickshaw right in front of Rajmahal. It was a two-storey building, with a restaurant on the ground floor and a new-looking neon sign running the length of the building that said

RAJMAHAL BAR AND RESTAURANT

Vimal paused for a moment, then walked in. The bill-clerk's counter was right next to the entrance. He walked up to the young man sitting there. The man looked up at Vimal.

"I want to meet Kaul," Vimal said curtly.

The bill-clerk looked Vimal up and down, frowning at his lack of respect.

"Regarding?" he asked.

Vimal glared at him, and said stonily, "Do I need to tell you?"

"Yes, you do."

Vimal was unnerved for a moment. "It's about Garewal."

"I don't get it."

"Your boss will."

"What's your name?"

"Vimal."

"Please take a seat," the clerk said, indicating a table past the counter.

Vimal went up to the table, pulled a chair, and sat down.

The clerk picked up the phone and began talking into it softly.

Vimal noticed that he hadn't dialled a number. That meant it was an extension telephone, and the other end—the main line—was definitely in the same building. He'd only pressed a buzzer button to signal he wanted to talk.

After a minute, the bill-clerk put down the phone. He rang a bell to summon a waiter. Gesturing towards Vimal, he gave the waiter some instructions. The waiter nodded and walked up to the table.

"Please come this way, sir," he said.

"Where?"

"To Kaul Saheb."

"All right."

Vimal stood up and followed him.

They crossed the restaurant and reached a narrow passage. There was a vestibule at the far end, from which stairs led up to the first floor. The two of them climbed up.

The waiter opened a door. It led to a drawing room. A man sat facing the door.

He was very thin, and so fair that he could have passed for an Englishman. He smiled a little at Vimal and said "Come in."

Vimal walked into the room.

"Have a seat."

He sat down.

"What did you say your name was?"

"Vimal."

"Oh, yes. Vimal. Vimal."

"And you're Kaul?"

"Yes. Will you have something to drink? Cold? Hot? Or even hotter?"

"No, I don't have the time."

"Okay. So come to the point. Which Garewal are you talking about?"

"You know perfectly well which Garewal I'm talking about. You're Harnam Singh Garewal's hired man."

Kaul scowled. Then he forced a smile again.

"Let me tell you this first," said Vimal. "I'm in the same business as Garewal—we're all playing the same game. We've never met, but I'm sure he'll have heard my name, the same way I've heard his."

"Your name? *I've* never heard it before."

"That's because I haven't told you the real one."

"And that is?"

"I've no intention of telling you. To you, I'm Vimal."

"What do you want?"

"I want information about a man who told me that he's worked with Harnam Singh Garewal. I want to find this man but I don't know how to get to him. I was hoping that Garewal might know. When I was asking about Garewal, I found out that you're his post office. And so I'm here."

"Who's this man you're looking for?"

"Mayaram Bawa. He'd said that he was better known in his line as Ustadji. Know him?"

"No. Why do you want him?"

"Just some reason."

"Which you don't want to tell me. So what you want me to do is ask Garewal whether he knows how to find Mayaram Bawa, alias Ustadji?"

"Or else let me meet Garewal myself. I'll ask him."

"That won't be possible," Kaul said with a show of apology. "But I can phone him."

"Fine."

"Anything else you wanted to ask?"

"No."

Kaul stood up.

"It'll take a while to phone. Have a drink while you wait."

"Make the phone call first."

Kaul went into the back room.

Vimal sat and waited, alert.

Shortly, he heard the sound of a phone being dialled, followed by Kaul's muffled voice. Vimal strained to make out the words, but could not.

Kaul returned in a while.

"I've left a message," he said, smiling again. "Garewal will call here soon."

"Thank you."

"Now tell me, what will you have?"

"Coffee will be fine," Vimal said.

Kaul walked out of the drawing room. Vimal heard him call out, "Oye Kalu, get two coffees!"

He came back in.

In a few minutes, a waiter brought in the coffees.

Vimal took a sip of the coffee and said, "How long do we wait for the phone call?"

"Half an hour at the most," Kaul said. "But it might come in five minutes."

"Where will he phone from?"

"What's your real name?"

Vimal went silent. He kept sipping at his coffee. For some reason, he was feeling uncomfortable.

"I'll be back," Kaul said, and went to the back room.

Vimal swallowed the last gulp of coffee and put down the cup. He straightened his legs and rested his back on the sofa cushion. His eyes felt heavy. Then suddenly he realized this was no ordinary drowsiness. He was falling unconscious.

He struggled to stand up. He shook his head to try to clear it, but it was spinning like a top; he felt like he was moving through water. He tried to call Kaul, but no sound came out.

A trick! Run!

He took a few steps towards the door, each foot feeling like it weighed a ton. Halfway there, he collapsed and fell to the floor.

He thought about the coffee he'd drunk, but before the thought was complete, he was out.

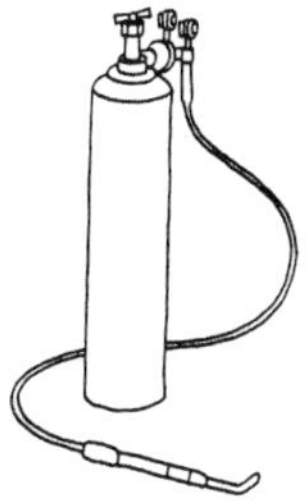

10

HE WAS SWIMMING. Diving deep into the sea. He was flying. Flying like a leaf among the clouds in the sky. Red and yellow stars danced before his eyes, fireworks burst into showers of stars.

His body seemed like a different creature. It refused to obey his commands. What had happened? What was happening?

Can you hear me?

He felt a sudden jerk to consciousness, then went floating again.

Can you hear me?

"Yes."

He found he could talk effortlessly. The answer slid easily off his tongue and flowed into the atmosphere.

Why are you looking for Mayaram Bawa?

"I'm looking for him."

Yes, but why?

"That bastard has run away with the loot. He killed two people too. He wanted to kill me. I escaped."

What loot?
"My loot. Our loot."

Who's 'us'?
"Karamchand, Labh Singh Matar-Paneer, Guranditta."

Where are they?
"All dead."

How did Bawa take your loot?
"Double-cross."

Where did the loot come from?
"The heist."

What heist? When?
"Saturday night."

Where?
"Bharat Bank. Lawrence Road. Amritsar. Punjab. India."

How much did you get?
"The newspaper. The newspaper has it."

How much?
"Sixty-five."

Lakhs?
"Yes."

Don't you know how to find Mayaram Bawa?
"No."

No address?
"Nothing."

But you'll still find him?
"Yes."

How?
"Harnam Singh Garewal. He has worked with Harnam Singh Garewal."

Any other way to reach Bawa?
"No."

Any friends? Anyone close to him?
"They're all dead."

So Garewal is your only means to reach Mayaram?

So Garewal is your only means to reach Mayaram? Answer me!
"Yes."

You have nothing against Garewal?
"No."

No quarrels? No grudges? You have nothing to do with him?
"Nothing."

If you don't get Garewal's help, will you be able to find Bawa?
"No."

Are you sure?
"Perhaps. Perhaps there's some other way."

What way?
"I don't know."

What will you do if you don't find Bawa?
"I'll do something. I'll find some other way."

What will you do?
"I'll do something."

What's your name?
"Sardar Surender Singh Sohal."

There was a silence.

Riding the winds. Floating in the clouds. Higher and higher. And higher.

Of Allahabad?
"Yes."

Any other name?
"Vimal Kumar Khanna of Mumbai."

And?
"Girish Mathur of Madras."

And?
"Banwarilal, the tonga-wala from Delhi."

And?
"Driver Ramesh Kumar, of Amristsar."

And?

And?

Mayaram Bawa has sixty-five lakhs?
"Yes."

Of what? Cash?
"Yes. Three big bags."

How did he get away?
"In a van."

With the sixty-five lakh rupees?
"Yes."

And you can't find him without Garewal's help?
"No."

Wonderful. Sat Sri Akaal, brother!

Silence.

The sky disappeared. The clouds disappeared. He fell into the roaring sea and sank lower and lower. His head wandered away somewhere. He splashed his arms around to get his head back and tried to join it to his body.

Silence.

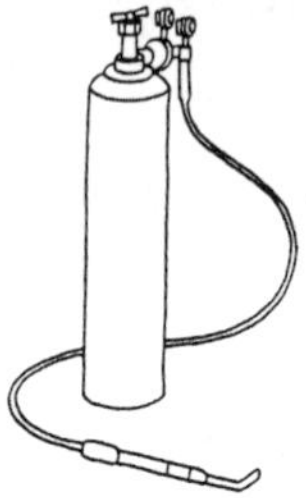

11

He opened his eyes blearily. All around was darkness. Where was he? His head hurt and he felt dizzy. He struggled to his feet, looking all around, trying to peer through the gloom. He was in a dark alley.

He staggered out to the main road. He was still on Queen's Road, but quite some distance from Rajmahal.

He smelled like a pig covered in muck. He looked at himself in the light. There were layers of mud caked on his clothes and skin, and he reeked of alcohol. When he'd been out, they'd splashed booze into his mouth and body and then thrown him into the gutter in the alley.

He felt a pain in his right arm. He rolled up his sleeve and saw a small wound there, a needle puncture. After he'd succumbed to whatever had been in the coffee, he must have been injected with some other drug, too.

He hailed a passing rickshaw.

"Ajit Nag—"

But the rickshaw-wala did not even wait for him to finish. He threw Vimal a disgusted glance and rode on.

Vimal looked through his pockets. He was relieved to find that they had not taken anything from him.

He stopped another rickshaw, and before the

rickshaw-wala could get a good look at him, he said, "Ajit Nagar. I'll give you five rupees."

The man looked at him suspiciously, but finally said, "Get in."

He climbed in quickly.

"Bauji," the rickshaw-wala said, "smells like you had a bath in the booze today."

Vimal didn't answer. He was still trying to stop his head from spinning.

One realization kept buzzing around his head, even as he sat in the rickshaw. The voice that had questioned him had not been Kaul's.

He got off some distance away from the bungalow in Ajit Nagar, and slipped into the house through the back door like a thief. He peeled off his clothes and threw them to the floor as soon as he reached his room, then went and stood under an ice cold shower.

When he came out of the bathroom, his body was trembling like a leaf, his teeth were chattering, and his lips were blue from the cold. But he felt better.

He put on a new set of clothes and sat down, wrapping himself in a thick blanket.

Just then, the old servant came in.

"Lalaji has asked you to take out the car." He said.

"All right. Can you do me a favour?"

"What?"

"Make me some hot tea."

"I'll get it."

Vimal took off his clothes again and changed into his driver's uniform.

The servant returned with a glass of tea.

Vimal swallowed four Anacins with the tea, then went downstairs. He drove the air-conditioned Lincoln out of the garage and stopped at the portico.

In a little while, the angel and the ape came out. He opened the back door for them, then slid back into the driving seat and asked, "Where to, saheb?"

"To Bhandari Saheb's house," the Lala said.

He drove to Maqbool Road. There were several cars parked outside Bhandari's house. A shamiana had been put up on the lawns, and a loudspeaker was blaring music. Some major function was going on.

Vimal sprang out of the car and opened the back door. The angel stepped out first, resplendent in gem-studded jewellery, and gave him a flirty glance before walking towards the house.

"We'll need two or two and a half hours here," the Lala said. "Have something to eat in the meantime."

"Yes, sir," he said deferentially.

The fat Lala waddled off, following his wife.

Vimal got back into the car and parked it. Lighting a cigarette, he tapped the steering wheel, thinking about what to do next.

When he had talked to Kaul, it had been daytime. By the time he'd regained consciousness, night had fallen. Which meant he had been out in the alley for several hours.

Who was the other man who had questioned him?

Garewal?

He decided to make another trip to Rajmahal. He might get some more information. Queen's Road was not far from here, and the Lala had said he would take at least two hours.

Vimal started the car and began to drive. He parked a short distance past Rajmahal. He placed his peaked cap on the seat behind him. His uniform only looked like a uniform because of the cap—without it, he was just a normal man wearing normal clothes.

He walked towards the restaurant and went in. Making sure not to look towards the bill-clerk's desk, he headed straight for the bar. The tables were almost full, and the bar was crowded, too. He found an empty stool and sat down. When the bartender came over, he ordered a peg of Whitefield.

"Where's the restroom?" he asked the bartender after emptying his glass.

The bartender indicated a door towards the back of the restaurant.

He headed towards it. When he pushed open the door, he found himself in the same narrow passage through which the waiter had led him to Kaul. It was empty. There were doors on either side of him, bearing signs reading LADIES and GENTS. Hesitating a little, he walked ahead. He reached the vestibule; it too was deserted. He stealthily began climbing the steps.

At the top, he found that the entrance to the flat had a large lock hanging from it.

Vimal took out a bunch of keys from his pocket. He tried every one that fit, but none of them turned. There was a nail cutter attached to the keyring, from which he pulled out the nail file. He worked it into the keyhole. After a little wiggling, the lock clicked open.

He went into the flat, shut the door, and drew the door curtain closed. Then he turned on the light in the drawing room. There was no window in the room, so the light wouldn't be seen from the outside.

He began to search.

There was a desk in the drawing room, with an ordinary lock that opened easily. He found a revolver, a torch, and a bundle of money in the drawers, all of which he put into his pockets without hesitation.

He opened the revolver and checked its chambers. It was fully loaded. He felt safer than he had when he'd broken in.

Using the torch, he made a thorough search of the flat.

There were two things missing.

First, there was no shaving kit in the bathroom—or anywhere else. Did Kaul get himself shaved at a barber shop? He didn't seem the sort.

Secondly, there was no suitcase in the house. But he found several bare clothes hangers in the cupboard in the bedroom. Kaul must have gone someplace.

There were clothes of two sizes in the wardrobe. There was also a starched turban. Did Harnam Singh Garewal live here too? The voice he'd heard when he was drugged was definitely not Kaul's. So had the questioner been Garewal?

He tried to remember the conversation.

He vaguely recalled being asked about the heist, the betrayal, and Mayaram Bawa. He'd also been asked whether he had any grudge against Garewal. The drug he'd been injected with had left him with no control over himself, so he must have replied truthfully to all the questions.

That meant that Garewal knew the whole saga too. What would he do? Would he try to warn Mayaram, or try to get the money for himself?

Both seemed equally likely.

One thing was for sure: Any chance of reaching Mayaram through Garewal was gone. Vimal would have to think of some other way.

In a cupboard in the bedroom, he found a half-filled injection bottle and a syringe. There was no label on the bottle, but he thought it must be the same drug that he'd been pumped with. He put both things in his pocket. Then he threw down the torch, turned off the light in the drawing room, and left the flat. He didn't try to relock the door.

He climbed down the stairs. At the turn, he paused and took a look around. The vestibule was still empty. He went back to the bar.

There was a public telephone booth in one corner of the room. He walked into it and closed the door.

He found the number of Rajmahal Restaurant in the directory and dialled it. It began to ring immediately. Through the glass of the booth, he could see the phone at the bill-clerk's desk. The clerk picked up the phone, and his voice came over the line. "Hello?"

"This is Sahni, from Delhi," Vimal said in a rough voice. "Is Kaul there?"

"He's not here, sir," the clerk said politely.

"Where has he gone?"

"He hasn't told anyone that."

"When will he be back?"

"He wasn't sure, but he said he would be back within a week."

"Did Garewal go with him?"

"Garewal who?"

"Harnam Singh Garewal."

"I don't know, sir."

"All right. When he returns, tell him Sahni called."

"Your phone number, sir?"

"He knows it already."

He hung up the receiver and walked out of the restaurant. Then he got into the car and turned back towards Maqbool Road.

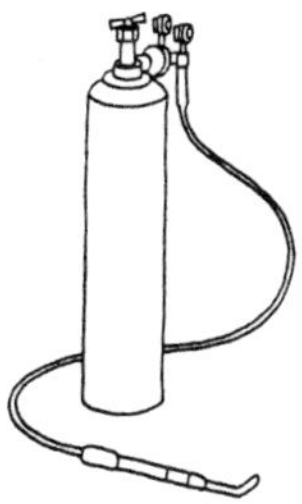

12

THE NEXT DAY'S PAPER had a photo of the van in which Mayaram had escaped. The police had found it near a bridge on the Beas River, abandoned. A laboratory check had revealed a few things:

There were no fingerprints of any kind on the van. It looked as if someone had taken great pains to clean it before leaving it there.

There was some flesh and blood on the tyres—more on the front tyres and less on the rear ones. Tests of the blood had revealed that it matched the two crushed bodies found near Khasa. Police experts had no doubt that this was the van used to kill the two men.

Now a connection could be made between the wrecked Fiat, the two bodies on the road, and the bank robbery. The theory was that the two crushed bodies and the accident victim were three of the five people involved. No one knew who the other two were, but it looked like they had murdered their three companions.

The fingerprints had not yet been traced, but the police spokesman said a report was due any day now.

Vimal knew that since he and Mayaram had been to jail and had police records, sooner or later, their fingerprints would be identified. Labh Singh's identity would also come out. He didn't know whether Guranditta or Karamchand had ever been to jail.

Clearly, the police were being very swift and efficient in their investigation.

Vimal spent the day asking around about Labh Singh, at all the places where he'd asked for Mayaram and Garewal earlier. It turned out that Labh Singh was better known by his nickname. Wherever he asked, more often than not, he'd get a response of "Which Labh Singh? Matar-Paneer?"

Many people had heard the name, but it took Vimal a while to find someone who had any useful information about him. This man told him that Labh Singh was a native of Jalandhar, was married, had children, and owned a house on a lane in Bhairon Bazaar in his hometown. Vimal noted down the address and, taking permission from Lala Haveli Ram, set out for Jalandhar by bus.

As the bus crossed the bridge over the Beas River, he thought again of Mayaram. If he'd left the van here, it was possible that he'd gone in the same direction. But all of India was in this direction; who knew where he was right now?

He reached Bhairon Bazaar in Jalandhar, and with a few questions he found Labh Singh's house quite easily. The building was ancient. Children shouted and played in the lane opposite the house. When he rapped at the door, the children's noise abated for a moment.

"Oye Sweety!" one kid yelled. "Someone's come to your house!"

The boy who'd been called Sweety was a Sikh lad, about ten years old. He cast a fleeting glance at Vimal, and hollered, "Bibi, someone's come!" Then, deciding he'd completed his duty, he turned away from Vimal and went back to his games.

Someone opened the window on the first floor of the house and looked out. A little later, the main door opened and a fat, barefoot woman appeared at the threshold.

Vimal folded his hands in greeting, and said in Punjabi, "My name is Vimal. I'm a friend of Labh Singh's."

An uncertain smile appeared on the woman's face.

"He's not at home," she said.

"I know. I came to talk to you."

"Kaka is not at home, either," she said hesitantly. "He's my eldest son, he—"

"Even if he were at home, I would want to talk to you."

"Oh! Come in, then."

Vimal went in. The house was quite clean inside, in much better condition than the outside. The woman led him to a courtyard. At her gesture, Vimal sat down in a cane chair.

"Will you have tea? Water?"

"No, that's all right. Please sit down."

She pulled up a cane stool and sat down.

"You're Labh Singh's wife?" Vimal asked.

She nodded.

"I'm sorry to say, I have some very bad news for you," Vimal said as gently as he could.

"Labh Singh's dead?"

Vimal stared at her. There was an strange expression

on her face; her eyes were empty. She seemed to be looking right through him.

"I can't say I'm very surprised," she said softly. "We've been married for twenty-two years. Ever since I found out what my Sardarji does for a living, I've been ready for this news. Every time he went out on any work, I'd have the terrible feeling that he wouldn't be back. It had to come true some time." She took a deep breath. "Evil deeds beget evil ends, Praaji! This hour had to come some day. That coward has left my children fatherless."

Two big tears rolled out of her eyes and fell onto her hands.

Vimal shifted restlessly.

When she wiped her eyes with her dupatta, more tears welled up. She managed to control herself after a while, and asked in a choked voice, "How did it happen?"

"He fell victim to a friend's treachery. Do you read the papers?"

"Yes."

"Then you'll have read the news about the heist on Bharat Bank, in Amritsar?"

"Labh Singh was part of that?"

"Yes."

"And you too?"

Vimal hesitated, then said "Yes."

"But the paper doesn't have anything about my Sardarji's death…"

"The news is there, but the police haven't identified the body yet. The two crushed bodies found near

Khasa—one of them was Labh Singh and the other was a man named Karamchand. Did you know him?"

She shook her head.

"The man who betrayed Labh Singh and crushed him under his van—his name was Mayaram Bawa. He called himself a childhood friend of Labh Singh. Do you know him?"

"I know him. Why did Bawa do this?"

"Because greed blinded him. Because dishonesty had taken root in his mind. Because he wanted all of the money from the heist for himself."

"How much?"

"Sixty-five lakhs. You must have read it in the paper."

"And you are looking for Bawa?"

"I want to punish him for his betrayal. I want to get that money back."

"And you don't know how to find him."

"But you do. I was sure you would know him. That's why I'm here."

"So if you'd been able to reach him some other way, you wouldn't have come to me at all? I'd never have known what happened to my Sardarji?"

"You are right. But that's not my fault. Labh Singh wasn't my friend; I hadn't even heard of him before all this happened. I didn't even know where he lived. How could I have felt any responsibility towards him?"

"Did he have a share?"

"Yes."

"How much?"

"About eleven and a half lakhs."

"I should get that money."

Vimal's lips curled in a bitter smile. "Behenji," he said, "Do you think loot from a robbery counts as inheritance?"

She was silent.

"And anyway, I don't have it. Mayaram vanished with it."

"But you're trying to get it back, aren't you?"

"I'm trying, yes. Why I'm doing it, you may not understand. But please try to believe this: I'm not doing it for the money. So don't expect me to deliver everyone's share door-to-door to their homes."

"But you can't get to Bawa without my help."

"So you're expecting Labh Singh's share as payment for your help?"

"I have five children," she said softly. "The man of the house has died and left nothing behind. There's no income. What can I do?"

Vimal felt a surge of sympathy. He fished out the bundle of notes he'd found in Kaul's flat and tossed it into the woman's lap.

"This is twenty-four thousand rupees," he said. "Make do with this. If I manage to get the money from Mayaram, I will try to get you something more. But please don't count on it."

She let the bundle lie, untouched, in her lap.

"Are you giving me this money from your pocket?"

"My pocket has never had anything in it." Vimal sighed. "I'm a poor man."

"So..."

"Forget it. Just eat the mangoes; don't count the trees."

She made no reply.

"Now let's come to the point."

"I don't know where Bawa lives these days."

"Then I came here for nothing," he said, disappointed.

"But I know a couple of people who could tell you his address," she quickly added. Her hand closed around the bundle of notes in her lap.

"Okay," Vimal said, without much enthusiasm. "Tell me about them."

"One of them lives here in Jalandhar," she said. "He has a cloth shop near Maam Naasar—Bajwa Cloth House. The owner, Attar Singh Bajwa, is a good friend of Mayaram's. He'll be able to tell you for sure."

"Who else?"

"There's a girl named Neelam. Lives in Chandigarh. The address is 2244, Sector 22-C, Chandigarh."

"Is she related to Mayaram?"

"About three years ago, Mayaram persuaded her to run away from home with him. That's the relation."

"Does Mayaram live with her?"

"Not now. He used to, until last year, then left. But I'm sure she'll know his current address."

"All right," he said, and stood up. The situation still seemed bleak. The information he'd gotten was vague, roundabout, and probably useless.

The woman remained seated, her head bowed.

"I'm going," he said, "but I have one request of you. Please don't talk about me to anyone."

"But I will have to go to Amritsar to identify my Sardarji. Otherwise how will I get the body? Won't those people ask me how I learned about his death?"

"Tell them you read about the recovery of an unidentified body in the papers. Your husband had gone to Amritsar and not returned. You came because you had a suspicion the body might be his."

"All right."

"And don't tell them that you knew what Labh Singh did for a living. Otherwise they'll keep bothering you."

"All right."

"I'm off. Sat Sri Akaal!"

"Sat Sri Akaal."

He returned to Bhairon Bazaar and began to walk towards Maam Naasar. He knew this area; it wasn't far away.

Bajwa Cloth House turned out to be a modern-looking store, with long counters and several salesmen. He found a salesman who didn't look too busy and asked for Attar Singh Bajwa. The salesman pointed towards a middle-aged Sikh sitting at the cash counter, surrounded by a wire cage for security.

Vimal went up to the counter and addressed the Sikh. "Bajwa Saheb?"

The man looked up. "Yes, please?"

"My name is Vimal. I want to talk to you for a minute."

"What about?"

"Mayaram Bawa."

"Come in."

Vimal lifted up the hinged section of the counter-top and went in. At a gesture from Bajwa, he sat down on a wooden stool next to him.

"What about Mayaram did you want to talk about?"

"Do you know Neelam?"

Bajwa looked at him doubtfully and then nodded.

"I'm her brother."

"Oh!" Bajwa looked at him with new interest.

"Mayaram's abandoned her. He's done her a great wrong. I'm looking for him, but I don't know his address. I heard that you would know where to find him."

"Who told you about me?"

"Labh Singh."

"Matar-Paneer?"

"Yes."

"You know him?"

"No, Neelam knows him. She met him in Chandigarh."

"Hmm." Bajwa was silent for a moment, thinking. "I don't know Mayaram's address now," he said, finally.

"I came to you with great hopes," Vimal said, pushing dejection into his voice.

"I'm really sorry, but I won't be able to help you."

"Do you know *anyone* who knows where he is?"

"No, I don't. But if you want to leave a message for him, tell me. If I ever get in contact with him, I'll let him know."

"No, there's no message. I wanted to meet him personally."

"In that case, sorry."

Vimal thanked him and left.

As soon as Vimal was gone, Bajwa lifted up the phone receiver and booked a P. & T. trunk call to Karnal, for a waiter named Amritlal.

Ten minutes later, the call was put through.

"Amritlal, this is Bajwa speaking. There's a message for Mayaram Bawa."

"Tell me, ji," the voice at the other end said.

"Tell him that a man named Vimal was looking for him. He said he was Neelam's brother—Neelam from Chandigarh."

"I'll tell him. Anything else?"

"That's it," Bajwa said and put down the phone.

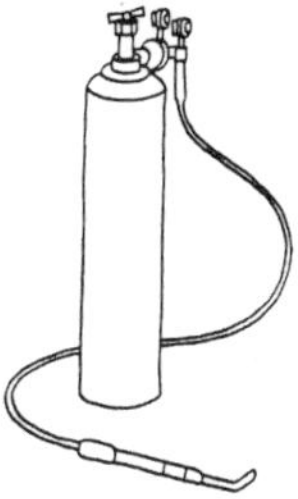

13

THE NEXT DAY, LALA HAVELI RAM had to leave abruptly for Delhi. From there, he would be travelling to Calcutta. He assured his wife that he would be back in a week.

That night Vimal was back in the wife's bed. They made full, acrobatic use of the luxurious bed until five in the morning. When it was time to leave, Vimal asked for three days off.

The Sethani was against it. She said that if he wanted time off, he should have taken it when the Lala was at home in Amritsar.

After a lot of begging and pleading, he managed to get his way—and managed to get one of the cars on loan, too.

Later that day, he took the Lala's new Ambassador and set out for Chandigarh. He was wearing a new suit that the Sethani had gotten made for him, and he looked dapper and high-class. He'd tucked the revolver that he'd found in Kaul's flat into his belt.

He had gotten into the habit of being ready to leave a place for good at a moment's notice, so he'd packed all of his belongings in his suitcase and brought it along. His hippie costume, his glasses, and the ten thousand in fifties he'd taken from the vault were in the suitcase too.

He reached Chandigarh at about one in the afternoon.

House number 2244 in Sector 22-C was easy to find. He rang the doorbell.

A beautiful girl wearing a Kashmiri gown opened the door. She appeared to have just woken up—it was a testament to the girl's beauty that she looked lovely in spite of that. She looked at Vimal with questioning eyes.

"Are you Neelam?" Vimal asked.

"Yes," she said warily.

"My name is Vimal. I'd like to talk to you."

"What about?"

"About Mayaram Bawa."

She hesitated. She looked Vimal up and down again, then said, "Go somewhere else. I haven't seen him for months."

"Where else do I go?"

"How would I know?" She tried to close the door.

"Listen," Vimal said hurriedly, sticking his foot in the opening.

"Move your foot," she said harshly.

"Look, I know you're angry with Mayaram—"

"How do you know?"

"I have probems with Mayaram too. People with a common enemy ought to make friends."

"How do you know that I'm angry at Mayaram?"

"The person who told me about you told me many things."

Neelam stopped to think. She looked at the car parked on the road. Looking back at Vimal, she asked, "Is that car yours?"

"Yes."

"Have you eaten?"

"No."

"Me neither. Can you take me out for lunch?"

"Sure. Anywhere you want."

"All right. Come in."

She moved away from the threshold. Vimal entered.

"What did you say your name was?"

"Vimal."

"Okay, Vimal. Sit here, I'll get ready."

"Okay."

She vanished into a door at the far end of the drawing room.

Vimal sat down on a sofa and lit a cigarette. The decor of the drawing room was impressive. Had Mayaram paid for all this? He really *was* used to quite a bit of luxury.

Getting to Mayaram seemed as difficult and slow as ever. He was groping his way around Mayaram's life like a blind man. It could backfire, too—Mayaram's acquaintances might warn him about a man asking too many questions.

Another thing he had to be careful of was not making the same mistake he'd made with Kaul. Instead of giving him anything, Kaul and Garewal had gotten information out of *him*—and now it looked like they were after Mayaram themselves. If he didn't find Mayaram before Garewal grabbed the loot, then what was the point?

Half an hour later, when Neelam came out, he stared at her open-mouthed. She looked too good to be true, delicate and alluring in the salwar-kameez and pullover she was wearing now. He felt a momentary rage at the thought that a bear like Mayaram had gotten her to elope with him and then lost interest in her.

"What is it?" Neelam was saying in her tinkling voice. "Is your mouth watering?"

"N-no," Vimal stuttered, and stood up.

"Come on, then, let's go."

They came out. Neelam locked her door, and they got into the car.

"Where to?" he said, turning on the ignition.

"Sona-Chandi."

"What sort of place is that?"

"It's a restaurant. Drive to the main road, I'll show you the way."

"Okay."

The car moved forward.

"You still haven't told me anything about Mayaram," Vimal said.

"What's the hurry?" she said. "I can't talk about serious issues on an empty stomach."

"So can I ask an ordinary question?"

"Ask."

"Did Mayaram really convince you to run away with him?"

Neelam looked at him, startled. "You really do know a lot about me."

"Not everything. Just a few things. You didn't answer my question."

"Yes. I really did run away with him."

"How did he do it?"

"I wanted to be a film star. He said he'd make me a heroine."

"But Chandigarh isn't the place for that sort of thing. You should've gone to Bombay."

"He did take me to Bombay at first. He really did make an effort, too, but nothing came of it. Actually, I was under the impression that he had a role for me, but it turned out that he was just planning to look for work on my behalf."

"So when it didn't work out, he brought you here to Chandigarh?"

"Yes. And kept me here in luxury."

"Then why did he leave you?"

"Must have gotten tired of me. That man has done me wrong. Now I can't go back home, can't do anything else."

"Didn't you try to find him?"

"I did try."

"So did you get him?"

"Now you're back on serious issues."

"Sorry."

They were silent for a few moments.

"So what do you do now?" Vimal asked abruptly. "I mean, how do you earn your living?"

"Give me five hundred rupees. You'll find out for yourself."

"I will. I can give you a lot more than five hundred. But I need to find what I'm looking for."

"What if I want five hundred before I talk?"

"Then I'll give you the money, get the information, and leave you here on the road."

"You mean no lunch?"

"No lunch."

"You're an evil man."

"Yes, maybe."

The restaurant turned out to be nearby, and the food was delicious.

When lunch was done and coffee was served, Vimal asked, "Shall we start on the epic tale of Mayaram?"

"Why are you looking for him?" she asked. "What's the story?"

"It's a long one."

"Which you don't want to tell me."

"Obviously."

"I haven't seen Mayaram for a year now."

"But you know where he lives?"

"In the car, you asked me whether I'd tried to find him. I told you I'd tried a lot. If I knew the bastard's house, would I have had to search for him?"

"So you don't know where to find him."

Neelam was silent.

Vimal took a deep breath. He looked at her helplessly, and finally said, "If you weren't so beautiful, I'd wring your neck."

"Go ahead, wring it," she said playfully.

"You did all this just to get a lunch out of me?"

"That's low," she said, suddenly turning serious. "It doesn't suit that face of yours."

He looked taken aback.

"I'll pay the bill," she said. "I'm not a beggar; it's not as if you're doing me a big favour by throwing me a roti. Look."

She opened her handbag and showed him. It was stuffed with hundred-rupee notes.

"Looks like you have many admirers in Chandigarh," Vimal said. "You've got plenty of people ready to pay your five hundred rupees. Do they have to wait in queue?"

"Yes. Do you want to queue up, too?"

"Is there any way to skip ahead?"

"Yes, but you can't afford it."

"Stop." Vimal put down his cup. "Enough chit-chat. I admit defeat and acknowledge that you're great at talk. Now tell me about Mayaram."

"I don't know where he lives."

"Maybe not, but you spent two years with him. You must know his friends and associates."

"I know a couple of them."

"Such as?"

"Labh Singh. He's a big fat Sardar—"

"Matar-Paneer?"

"Yes, that's him. You know him?"

"Forget about him. Tell me about someone else."

"Krishnamurti."

"Who's that?"

"He's another friend of Mayaram's. He used to visit here sometimes. He has a hotel named New Madras Hotel in Patiala, which is less of a hotel and more of a hangout for thieves and dacoits."

"He's a South Indian?"

"Yes. A Madrasi. Huge. Black as a cobra."

"Anyone else?"

"Once or twice I heard Mayaram talk about someone named Amritlal. It sounded like he was a good friend. He used to live in Chandigarh. I don't know where he is now, but he's definitely not here."

"No clue how to find him?"

"None."

"Anyone else?"

"There's an inspector in Kapurthala—Amrik Singh Gill. He too was a good friend of Mayaram's. Whenever he came to Chandigarh, he stayed with us."

That's useless, he thought. *How can I ask a police inspector for Mayaram's address?*

"Anybody else?"

Neelam thought for a few seconds, then shook her head.

"Think carefully."

"No, no one else."

"If he's in danger, do you think he'd come to you for help?"

"I wish he would. If I see that bastard, I'll scratch out his eyes."

"But would he come?"

"Perhaps. There's no way to be sure. If all other routes are closed to him, he might knock on my door."

"Hmm."

"You seem really anxious to get to him."

"Yes."

"What's the story?"

"I'll tell you some other time. If we happen to meet again, we'll have a lot to talk about. But first, I need to get my hands on that Mayaram."

"You're very angry at him?"

"Yes."

"What'll you do if you catch him?"

"Beat him so hard he'll beg for mercy."

"Do that. Deal him a few from me, too."

"Fine."

"Listen." Suddenly she was conspiratorial. "If Mayaram comes to me, I'll let you know. All right?"

"All right. That would be very good of you."

"And if I think of some other acquaintance of his, I'll tell you that too."

"Thank you."

"Give me your address."

"I don't have a fixed address, but I plan to be in Chandigarh for the next couple of days. I'm staying at Aroma. In the meantime, if you think of anything, give me a call there. If I'm not in, leave a message for me with the receptionist."

"Where will you go after the couple of days?"

"Amritsar. When I go there, I'll tell you where I'm staying."

"Why don't you stay with me?"

"Not now. I'll come to you when I can afford your services without having to stand in queue."

"Oh, stop the jokes."

"I wasn't joking. If I get hold of Mayaram, I'll not only be able to afford your special rate, but I'll book you for so long that you'll have to turn all your other customers away."

"Okay!" She grinned. "I'll be waiting for that day."

When the bill came, they quarrelled over who would pay. Finally, Vimal managed to pay it himself.

What had the girl seen in him, he wondered?

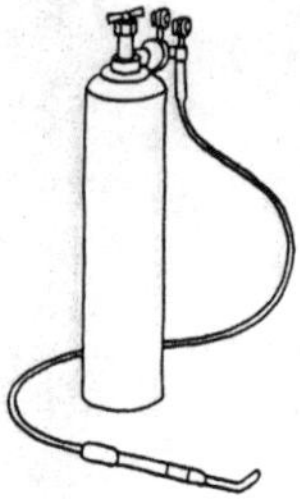

14

MAYARAM WAS FRUSTRATED that Vimal had gotten away, but now he was out of his grasp and there was nothing he could do about it. He should have pretended to leave, then parked the van past the turn and come back to gun Vimal down.

What was done was done, though. Vimal had escaped.

But, he thought, Vimal wouldn't be able to do much now. He didn't know where Mayaram lived; how could he find him? There was no way. Working on his own without any help in such a huge country, where would he look? Anyway, there was a good chance that he'd be caught by the police soon.

In that case, the thorn would be gone from Mayaram's flesh.

Still, it was in his best interests to stay undercover for the next few days. Vimal might not be able to find him, but why take the risk? If Vimal got caught, then the police would also find out that Bawa had been involved in the heist. He'd made a mistake there, too, he realized—he shouldn't have given Vimal his real name.

But the question now was, where should he hide?

He thought of Krishnamurti, but he dropped the idea quickly. Krishnamurti was his old friend. Anyone asking after Mayaram was sure to reach him. And he was a weasel, that Madrasi. If he found out the whole truth, he'd forget all about friendship and try to get the loot himself.

Then he thought of Neelam. It had been a year since he'd left her. Perhaps no one would think of her in connection with him. The girl was mad at him, but he was sure he could handle her. Money could smooth over the worst of arguments. But what if she'd changed in the past year? He'd cheated her. She might want to take revenge on him, to deceive him in turn.

Amritlal?

No. Everyone in his circle knew that Amritlal was his post office. Anyone looking for Mayaram would try Amritlal first.

Then he thought of Kailash Kumar Khanna.

Khanna had been his classmate in school in Ludhiana. Mayaram had left off studying after high school, but Khanna had gone to college and now had a high post in a company in Delhi.

Mayaram had been the leader of his gang in school, and Khanna had been his loyal chamcha. After finishing school, Khanna had moved to another town, so the two had not seen each other for many years. When they'd finally met again, Mayaram sensed that Khanna still respected him the way he had in their school days. That day, quite by coincidence, Mayaram had been wearing expensive clothes, and Khanna had assumed without asking that he was doing well in life. To keep the illusion intact, Mayaram had boasted of owning a motorcycle parts plant in Singrur. Khanna had given him his card and told him to visit if he ever came to Delhi.

They had met on two or three other occasions after that, and Khanna had told him every time to come to his place when he was in Delhi. A businessman like him, Khanna had said, must have to come to Delhi frequently; perhaps he felt awkward and was deliberately avoiding his home? Mayaram had assured him every time that he'd definitely come on his next visit.

He searched through his pockets and came up with the creased, dirty card that Khanna had given him. It listed an address in Nizamuddin.

Mayaram decided he would hide out at Khanna's house. Khanna was a respected man and belonged to high society. No one would imagine that Mayaram would be on close terms with a man of such stature.

He arrived in Delhi. Khanna's house in Nizamuddin was a picture-perfect bungalow. It was so neat and well-maintained that it made Mayaram feel a little nervous stepping into it.

Khanna was at home. His face lit up when he saw Mayaram. Mayaram told him straightaway that he planned to spend a few days in Delhi. He said he'd quarrelled with his wife and had left home to get some peace and quiet. He described his imaginary family as if it were some piece of bad luck, and said it would be a blessing to get away from them for a while. He began to talk of staying in a hotel—but Khanna stopped him and said he would be happy to have him.

Mayaram's three suitcases were carried into the guest room. Two of them were stuffed with the loot from the heist, and were locked securely.

Khanna introduced Mayaram to his wife Kiran and his three children. Kiran looked as beautiful as a film actress, and definitely too young to be a mother of three, even though her eldest son was ten years old.

After meeting Khanna's family, Mayaram felt a twinge of regret for being a criminal, an unwanted part of society. If he hadn't taken up with the wrong company, he too might have been a respectable man today. Then he reminded himself that he had sixty-five lakh rupees in his luggage. In today's society, respect was something one could buy.

He settled in.

From the first day, he could feel that regardless of the respect his friend might have for him, Khanna's wife didn't particularly like him. He'd seen it on her face several times. But he didn't give it much thought. He was here for a reason—who cared what his host's wife thought of him?

He tried to make friends with the children, but they didn't seem to like him much either. He couldn't become their "Uncle ji."

During the daytime, when Khanna went to his office, Mayaram felt like an unwelcome visitor in the house. Kiran did the minimum possible to remain the polite hostess, talking to him only when it was required and ignoring him completely when it wasn't. Mayaram pretended not to notice.

He made a call to Karnal, gave Amritlal the phone number of Khanna's house, and said he could reach him there until further notice. He didn't tell Amritlal where the house was.

He read the newspaper every day. It was rather frightening to see the speed at which the investigation was proceeding. He almost lost his nerve when he read about the fingerprints recovered from the aluminium ladder. He felt danger looming over him. Once the investigation into the prints was complete, his photograph would be in the paper, and the Khanna family would know that he was a criminal, not a businessman. These people, who were treating him as a guest, would become a threat. Then he'd have to get away immediately.

Amritlal called him two times on Wednesday.

The first time was in the morning, to let him know that Harnam Singh Garewal was asking questions about him. Garewal was spreading the word in criminal circles that he wanted to meet Mayaram because he had a big scheme cooking that would make him lakhs. Anyone who met Mayaram was to tell him that.

But Mayaram already had lakhs. He had no intention of ever doing another job for the rest of his life. He ignored the message.

However, a seed of doubt was growing in his mind. Was it possible that Garewal had found out that he had the loot from the Bharat Bank heist? In that case, wouldn't he be trying to squeeze it out of him? Maybe this rumour of a big scheme was just a ruse.

No, that wasn't possible, Mayaram decided. There was no way Garewal could know about the heist, and definitely no way he could know that Mayaram had all the loot.

In the evening, Amritlal called again. He told him that someone named Vimal had been asking about him.

Mayaram was silent for a moment. "Who told you this?" he asked.

"Attar Singh Bajwa, from Jalandhar," was the answer.

"Did he say anything else?"

"No, that was all. I thought I should tell you."

"You did well."

He slowly put the receiver down, and held his head in his hands. Fate worked in strange ways, he thought. The heist was supposed to be the difficult part, but it had mostly gone smoothly. Now these little things loomed like mountains in front of him.

God strike this Vimal! How had he got to Attar Singh Bajwa? He must have found Labh Singh's wife.

But Vimal couldn't have obtained any useful information from Bajwa. Bajwa didn't know anything about Mayaram except how to contact his middleman.

What if Labh Singh's wife had told Vimal about some of Mayaram's other friends? No—she didn't know many. And even then, none of his friends knew his current address or had any way of finding out.

Mayaram relaxed a little. Let the bastard try and find him. When it's time for a jackal to die, he runs toward his death.

He sat by the phone, trying to convince himself.

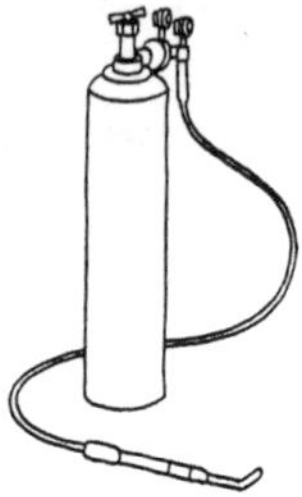

15

THE RESTAURANT WHERE AMRITLAL worked remained open till one a.m. Amritlal lived close by, and was walking home, hands in his pockets.

It was rather cold, but he didn't mind it. He'd earned a good tip from work today, and a hundred rupees from Ustadji as well.

Mayaram Bawa paid him fifty rupees for every phone call he made. Sometimes it would be weeks before he earned a fifty, but today he'd had occasion to call twice.

Amritlal lived by himself in a single room; his family was in Nakodar. He wanted to get married, but there was no question of it before he had at least ten thousand rupees saved up. He was happy to be moving closer to his target.

He was friendly with the bartender, who tonight had skimmed a little from the customers' drinks and given Amritlal two pegs of brandy. He felt a warm glow from the drink, and mumbled a little prayer to Bhagwati Bhavani as he walked home.

He unlocked his door and went in. Turning on the light, he walked into the kitchen. He usually drank a glass of warm milk before going to sleep. He heated the milk on the stove and poured it into a brass tumbler. Switching off the light in the kitchen, he came out into the hall.

There was a huge Sikh sitting in the single chair in the room, holding a gun. A slim, fair Kashmiri stood next to him.

The tumbler of milk fell from Amritlal's hand and clanged on the floor. Milk splattered at his feet. His eyes widened with terror at the gun-toting Sikh.

He knew the man.

His name was Harnam Singh Garewal and he was a dangerous gangster, well-known throughout Punjab. He had come by a few days earlier asking questions about Mayaram Bawa, but at the time Amritlal had told him that he knew nothing of Bawa's location.

Shera Waliye, he thought, praying to Bhagwati. Dealing with Bawa had finally landed him in trouble.

Garewal got up. He handed the gun to the young man standing next to him and stepped up to Amritlal.

Amritlal's tongue felt stuck. He tried to speak, but no sound came out. Garewal seemed as big as a mountain and wilder than a tiger.

"Are you married?" Garewal said softly.

Amritlal quickly shook his head, still unable to talk.

"That's good. Some girl's been saved from being widowed."

Amritlal began to shake like a leaf.

Garewal extended a giant hand and grabbed his throat.

"You son of a bitch," Garewal said menacingly. "You had the gall to lie to me!" His red eyes bulged. "Everyone I asked told me that you're the only one who knows where Mayaram is. And yet you told me you didn't! Why did you lie? Why?"

"Let go of his throat, at least," Kaul said calmly. "How will he speak?"

Garewal loosened his hold a little, but didn't let him go.

"Talk!" he growled. "Where is Bawa?"

"I don't know!" Amritlal mewled. "I swear by Bhagwati Bhavani, I don't know!"

Garewal's other hand crashed into his nose. At the same time, he let go of his neck.

Amritlal's body flew up and slammed into the wall. Blood spurted from his nose and his head felt like a spinning top. Garewal grabbed him by the collar and jerked him to his feet.

"Where is Bawa?" he asked again, grinding his teeth.

"I don't know!" Amritlal was in tears. "By the name of Wahe Guru, I don't know!"

"Bastard, how dare you take Wahe Guru's name in a lie! I'll tear you limb from limb! I'll drink your blood!"

And he began to beat Amritlal as though he were a bale of cotton.

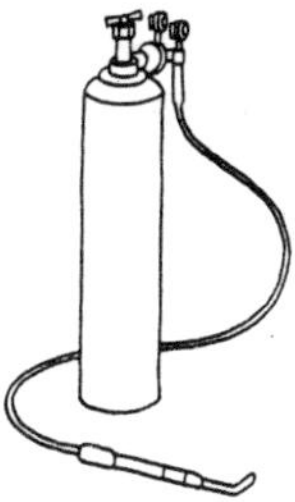

16

"THANK GOODNESS HE'S GONE," Kiran said, "I hope he never comes back."

"I'm praying for the same thing myself," Khanna said. "Not because I have any complaint against him, but at least it'll stop your constant bitching."

"Think of the children at least," Kiran said, making a face. "I've told you a thousand times not to use such language in front of them. They'll start using it themselves."

Khanna stopped, subdued.

They were seated at the table, having dinner. He glanced at the children, then said sternly to his eldest son, "Kamal, chew your food properly."

Kamal didn't raise his head.

They continued to eat in silence.

Kiran had been out of the house on an errand and Khanna hadn't yet returned from work when Mayaram had left. They found a note in the drawing room saying that he'd had to leave urgently on some important work, and could not meet them before going away.

When they looked through the guest room after dinner, they found that Mayaram had taken only one of his suitcases with him. The other two were still in the large cupboard.

That meant he hadn't left for good. He would be back, if only to collect his luggage.

Kiran hadn't liked Mayaram one bit. She thought he looked like a thief, a total lowlife. Khanna's opinion of him was slowly changing, too. He'd started to get the feeling that Mayaram was not worthy of the respect they were giving him. If Kiran hadn't taken a dislike to him, he probably would have told him they couldn't put him up anymore, and arranged for him to stay at a hotel. But since Kiran kept complaining, Khanna had continued to tolerate him—because he didn't want to feel cowed by his wife.

After the children had gone to sleep, Khanna went to his bedroom. Kiran came in a few minutes later.

"I looked through the Punjab telephone directory, you know," she said. "There's no motorcycle factory in Singrur owned by any Mayaram."

"How did you look it up? He's never told us the name of his factory."

"I looked through all the factories in Singrur. None of them mention Mayaram's name. And anyway, Mayaram Bawa's name isn't in the directory. Wouldn't a big man like him have a telephone at home?"

"He must keep his number unlisted."

"And the factory?"

"He must have kept his name out of that, too. There must be some reason."

"You keep coming up with excuses for him, but you refuse to listen to me," Kiran said, annoyed. "Look, you could come up with a thousand explanations, but they won't convince me. I'm sure he's some sort of criminal."

"All right, if you say so. But he's still a friend of mine. If he's behaving respectably with us, what does it matter what he is?"

"Mark my words: One day he'll clean out this house, too."

"If he planned to do that, why didn't he do it today? Today he had a good chance."

Kiran fell silent.

"In fact, he's even left his luggage here!"

"We should see what's in those suitcases," Kiran said, with new enthusiasm.

"Why?"

"To find out the truth. Who knows, he might be a smuggler! It might be ganja, or heroin, or cocaine, or something! Maybe he left it here to get us into trouble!"

"Looks like you're reading too many spy novels."

"Don't joke!"

"We can't open them. It would be impolite."

"To hell with politeness!"

"And anyway, the suitcases are locked."

"We can try to open them. Maybe some key in the house will work."

"Kiran, don't get after him like this. Whoever that man is, he's a friend of mine. I—"

Just then, the telephone rang. They stopped and looked at each other.

"I'll get it," Kiran said and went into the drawing room.

She was back immediately.

"Sounds like it's him," she said, as if telling him a secret. "Wants to talk to you."

Khanna stood up doubtfully. He went to the drawing room. Kiran was waiting in the doorway.

Khanna put the receiver to his ear and said uncertainly, "Hello?"

It was Mayaram at the other end. He sounded scared and out of breath.

"Khanna!" he said, "There's been some trouble here—"

"Trouble?" Khanna said. "What sort of trouble?"

"I can't come back to your place. There's a big problem here. I'm—"

"Where are you calling from?"

"Karnal. There's a friend of mine here. Someone beat him badly, almost killed him. He's in really bad shape. I need to be with him now; he'll die if I don't help him. After that, I'll leave."

"Leave for where?"

"I haven't decided yet. But wherever I go, I'll keep in touch with you."

"Okay…"

"Now the problem is those two suitcases that I've left at your place. You need to hide them somewhere safe."

"H-hide them?" Khanna stuttered.

"Yes, and don't tell your wife where. Just do it quietly."

"But Kiran is—"

"Look, I'm telling you this for her own good. It's best that she know nothing about all this. A man might come there, asking about me."

"What?"

"It's nothing to worry about. I'll tell you right now what you have to say to him."

"But what do you mean? Who's going to come here?"

"The friend of mine who's been beaten up—I'd given him your number. Someone has forced the number out of him. Now that man—"

"My phone number! My God, what mess have you gotten me into?"

"It won't be anything, I swear. Just listen to me. It's possible no one will contact you, but if anyone does, just tell them this: You used to know me a long time ago. One day, out of the blue, I called you and asked you a favour: If anyone phoned with a message for me, then you were to pass it on to me. You agreed. Since then, you have received two messages. One was that Harnam Singh Garewal was asking for—"

"I can't do all this."

"Just do as I say, Khanna! Do you want to end up in the same situation as my friend in Karnal?"

"What is this man after? Your suitcases?"

"No! He's only interested in me. Forget all that. Just remember that you took two messages for me. Then, after a while, I called and you gave me the two messages. That is all you know. You don't know where I am or where I was calling from. Understand?"

Khanna looked at Kiran in the doorway. She was looking at him, frightened.

"If I call the police, then—"

"Don't do that! Even by mistake!" Mayaram said sharply. "Or you'll be in worse trouble. You'll be arrested for harbouring an escaped criminal."

"What?"

"It's nothing to worry about, Khanna! It's possible that he won't even come there. Just take the suitcases and hide them properly, immediately. And if he comes, tell him the story I just told you. He'll believe you; he has no reason to doubt it. Then he'll go away and never show his face again. All right? Are you listening?"

"I'm listening," Khanna said, licking his suddenly dry lips.

"Now listen to the messages carefully and memorize them."

Mayaram told him the messages, the times at which they had come in, the caller's name, and the time Mayaram had supposedly called Khanna to get them. Then he asked Khanna to repeat it all. He sounded relieved when Khanna got it all right on the first try.

"I'll call you in a couple of days," Mayaram said, finally. "And don't worry about anything. Nothing's going to happen to you."

The line was disconnected.

Khanna stood for a while listening to the dial tone. Kiran was looking at him. He knew that as soon as he put the receiver down, he was going to have countless questions to answer.

A thousand thoughts went through his head as he stood there with the receiver to his ear.

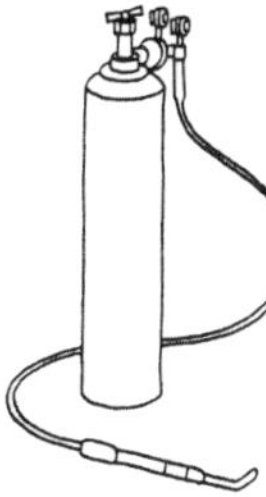

17

A PUBLIC TELEPHONE BOOTH stood a few buildings away from Khanna's bungalow in Nizamuddin. Harnam Singh Garewal left Kaul standing in front of the bungalow and went to the booth. He'd given the gun—fitted with a silencer—to Kaul with instructions to shoot Mayaram Bawa in the leg if he came out of the bungalow.

It was eleven p.m.

They had reached Delhi before noon that day. It had taken them an hour to get hold of the address matching the telephone number that the waiter had given them. They'd spent the day watching the bungalow, hoping they'd catch Mayaram Bawa coming out, or see him through the window. No such luck. They still had no way of being sure whether Mayaram was really there, or whether Amritlal had lied to them.

They hadn't really given Amritlal the option of lying, though. Garewal had given him a brutal thrashing. If Kaul hadn't stopped him, he'd probably have beaten him to death. Garewal had a foul temper. He had refused to believe that Amritlal didn't know where Mayaram was. The repeated denials had made Garewal angrier and angrier, and he had lashed out even more violently. Finally Kaul had forcefully pulled Garewal away, then talked to Amritlal himself in a gentler tone. The badly bruised waiter had burst into tears and told him that he knew nothing but a telephone number in Delhi.

Kaul persuaded Garewal that the man must be speaking the truth—as it was, they had no choice but to believe him. No one could hide anything after such a beating.

So they had come to Delhi.

Garewal and Kaul made an odd pair. Garewal was a mountain of a man, with violent eyes and a brutal, cruel face. In contrast, Kaul was delicate and fair, with finely chiselled features and a feminine grace. People initially speculated about their relationship, cooked up obscene ideas. Once, Garewal had heard one of them speculating. The next morning, the corpse of the man had been found floating in the canal near Chativind. After that, no one dared to talk.

Garewal went into the booth and dialled the number.

The phone rang for a long time. Finally someone picked it up, and a suspicious voice said, "Hello?"

"Please call Mayaram to the phone, ji," Garewal said, trying to keep his voice as courteous as possible.

A sharp exhalation came over the line, and then silence. Then the voice spoke hurriedly, "There's no Mayaram here. You've dialled the wrong number."

"No. The number is right. I want to talk to Mayaram Bawa."

"There's no one with that name here." There was a tremor in the voice.

Had Mayaram grown suspicious? Had he slipped away? It was quite possible, Garewal thought. "I want to talk to him. Is there any way I can reach him?"

"I don't know. I don't know any Mayaram Bawa."

If the man was telling the truth, why was his voice shaking? Why was he frightened?

"Look, Bauji," he said. "My name is Harnam Singh Garewal. I'm a friend of Mayaram's. Just last night, Amritlal called this number from Karnal and spoke to Mayaram. Now I want to talk to him myself."

"Harnam Singh Garewal?"

Garewal hesitated. Perhaps he shouldn't have given his name. But then, Mayaram had no reason to shy away from him. Mayaram had no way of knowing that Garewal had gotten the whole story out of Vimal, and already knew about the loot.

"Yes," he said, "Mayaram and I are old friends."

"Harnam Singh Garewal," the voice said again, uncertainly. "He'd mentioned that name to me."

"He must have. He's a friend of mine."

"But he's not here now and I have no idea where he is. If you want to leave a message, then—"

"When did he leave your place?"

"Leave? He's never come here."

Another lie. Hadn't he just said he wasn't there *now*? That meant he had been, earlier.

"But he'll be calling here," the voice continued. "If you want to leave a message for him, give it to me."

"Yes. Tell him I called."

"Any number where he can reach you?"

"No. Just tell him that Garewal called, and wants to get in touch."

"All right."

Garewal put the phone down.

He came out of the booth and walked towards the bungalow, deep in thought.

Could it be that the telephone number was just another link in the chain leading towards Mayaram? Perhaps Amritlal left messages here for Mayaram to pick up later? But it was clear that Mayaram had been here at some point...

He reached Kaul, and looked at him questioningly.

Kaul shook his head.

Garewal turned to look at the bungalow.

"What did you find out?" Kaul asked, "Is he inside?"

"Looks like he isn't," Garewal said. "But he was, not too long ago. Khanna is sure to know where he's gone. Let's go in."

The two moved forward. Instead of going straight towards the building, they walked around the side of the bungalow where a telephone cable ran along the top of the wall. Garewal lifted Kaul up onto it; Kaul pulled a small knife from his pocket and cut the wire.

Then Garewal too climbed onto the wall. Stealthily, they jumped into the compound. There was a garage to the side of the bungalow with its rolling shutter raised halfway. They ducked in, and Garewal brought the shutter down after them.

Garewal felt along the wall, found a switch, and turned the light on. In the dim light, they saw a door with a glass window at the far end of the garage. They walked over and looked in. They could see the kitchen.

Garewal pulled out the pistol tucked into the drawstring of his pajama, and shattered the glass with the butt. Putting his hand through the broken glass, he drew the bolt and pushed the door open. The two went in. Light from the drawing room spilled into the kitchen. They closed the door through which they'd come in. Just then, they heard footsteps. They stiffened, tightening their grips on their guns.

A man appeared in the kitchen doorway. He wore a pajama suit, a woollen gown, and slippers. Noticing them, he stopped, and stared at them with widening eyes.

"Who are you?" he said, fear in his voice. "What are you doing here?"

Garewal immediately recognized the voice from the telephone conversation. "You're Khanna?" he asked.

Khanna didn't answer. He put out a hand and flicked a switch. The kitchen flooded with light.

"Kaul," Garewal said, "take a look around the house."

"Stop!" Khanna said. He moved as if to block Kaul's way.

Garewal raised the hand holding the gun, and Khanna noticed for the first time that they were armed. He froze. Kaul walked out of the kitchen. Garewal and Khanna stood there, waiting. A moment later, they heard a woman's angry voice and a crying child. Khanna opened his mouth to say something, but at a fierce glare from Garewal, he kept quiet.

Then Kaul's voice sounded. "All clear, Sardar!"

"Move," Garewal said, waving the gun at Khanna. They walked out.

Kaul was in the drawing room. He'd closed the windows and doors and pulled the curtains. A woman sat on the sofa, along with three children. She looked scared, yet defiant. The children sat huddled with teary eyes.

"There was someone staying in the guest room," Kaul said, "but I think he's gone now. There's no luggage or anything."

"That means he won't be back," Garewal said. He looked at Khanna and the woman questioningly. "Right?"

"He won't come back here!" the woman said sharply. "We don't want him here—or you!"

"Kiran!" Khanna warned.

"You keep quiet, ji. All this trouble is your doing."

Khanna shut up. He looked uncertainly at Garewal.

"Bau," Garewal said, "I called you a little while ago."

"You're Garewal!" Khanna exclaimed.

"Yes. Harnam Singh Garewal." He stroked his moustache with his free hand. "I'm sorry to have to bother you folks so late at night. But I had no choice. I need to talk to Mayaram Bawa as soon as possible. All you need to do is tell us where he's gone. After that we'll leave."

"But we don't know where he's gone," Khanna said. "I'm telling the truth, I know nothing."

"Then you're in real trouble," Garewal said with mock regret, "because we aren't leaving without finding out. If you really don't know, then we're going to be your guests for a long time."

"He said he'd telephone," Khanna said helplessly. "That's all he said. Nothing about where he was or where he was going, I swear to God. But he'll call for sure."

"Then you're in even worse trouble," Garewal said. "We've cut your telephone cable. I guess we'll have to wait for him to come back."

For a second, an expression crossed Khanna's face, which confirmed Garewal's suspicion that Mayaram would return. Khanna looked away and licked his lips.

"Yes, that sounds right," Garewal said in a satisfied tone. "He'll be back. What do you think, Bau saheb, when do you think he'll come?"

"He won't," Khanna said. "He said he'd telephone. When he can't get through, he'll get suspicious and stay away."

"I don't think so. I think he'll just assume the phone's out, and then he'll come here for sure. We'll all wait here for him—that is, unless you remember something about where he went."

"I have no idea. I swear to you, I don't know."

"Listen," Kiran said suddenly to her husband. "If you want to protect that man, then—"

"My God, what nonsense! You think I care for him more than my own wife and children?"

Garewal looked at Kiran and pushed his face into something wasn't quite a smile. "Kaki, your man might not know—but perhaps *you* know something."

"I haven't talked to him," Kiran said. "When he called, my husband answered."

"He called?" Garewal whirled towards Khanna. "When was this?"

"This evening."

"Did he say where he was calling from?"

"He said he was in Karnal, but leaving soon... Something about someone beating up his friend."

"Hmm," Garewal looked at Kaul. "So he got to Karnal, the son of a bitch."

Kaul nodded.

"What do you think, will he be back?"

"It's hard to say," Kaul said. "The phone line's cut. That might make him suspicious."

"It's just a wire. Patch it up."

"All right."

"That's better. We'll fix the phone line and then wait here. Bauji, if Mayaram calls, tell him everything's fine here, he can come back, no problem. Say it confidently. We don't want him getting suspicious."

"Okay," Khanna said weakly.

"Shall I fix the phone now?" Kaul said.

"No, wait a bit. For now, just keep a lookout. And Kaki," he said, giving Kiran a fiendish smile, "why don't you give me a little tour of the house?"

Kiran shrank away from him. She stared, terrified, at his gorilla-like face.

"Sardar," Kaul said under his breath. "Don't."

Garewal laughed.

"Nothing to worry about," he said. He turned towards Kiran again. He moved a hand toward her and said, "Come on, show me the rest of the house."

"Stop!" Kiran shrieked. "Don't touch me!" She pulled away.

Garewal tried to grab her arm. Kiran slapped his hand away. Garewal's face turned purple with rage.

"You...you..." he said in a voice quivering with anger. He smacked Kiran so hard she fell back onto the sofa. The slap echoed in the room as if a bomb had gone off.

One of the children began to cry loudly. The other two stared, speechless.

Khanna yelled, and lunged at Garewal.

In a split second, Garewal reached forward and grabbed him as if he were a stuffed toy. With his left hand wrapped around Khanna's throat, he began to methodically pummel him with his right.

When Harnam Singh Garewal lost his temper, he turned into a demon.

Overleaf: Advertisement for "Surender Mohan Pathak's *Ghaatak Goli* (The Fatal Bullet), from Raja Pocket Books."

हन पाठक

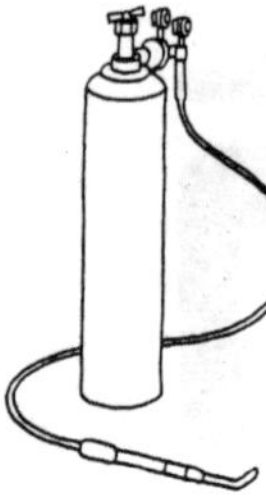

18

THE RINGING OF THE DOORBELL woke Neelam. At first she thought she was dreaming, but then she realized it was real. There was someone at her door. She looked at the radium dial of the clock on the side table; it was two a.m.

Who could it be at this hour? she wondered.

She thought of Vimal. His handsome, friendly face swam before her eyes and a strange hope arose in her mind. She began to imagine how, when the door opened, he would take her into his arms, shower kisses on her lips and face, then carry her into the bedroom. But then she stopped fantasizing. Why would Vimal come at this hour? For sex? No, impossible. He didn't seem like the sort of man who would lose his head over a woman. Who could it be, then?

The bell rang again. She switched on the light and got up. Her nightgown lay at the foot of the bed. She picked it up and began to pull it on. *Perhaps an old customer*, she thought as she walked towards the door. Just before she opened it, Mayaram's face flashed before her eyes. A shudder ran through her body. *Oh God, what if Mayaram has found out that I am helping an enemy of his?* She felt a stab of fear.

The bell was ringing continuously. Whoever it was, she would have to open the door.

"Who is it?" she called out.

"It's me, Mayaram," the voice came. "Open up."

Neelam opened the door apprehensively .

Mayaram burst in.

But he didn't look angry. He looked terrified. His eyes darted restlessly about the room. He threw down the suitcase he was carrying, turned back to the door, and quickly locked it from the inside. "What happened?" he asked her. "You took a month to open the door."

She said nothing. She felt a fleeting twinge of guilt at the thought that she'd conspired to betray this man.

Mayaram looked around and then said, "Is there someone in the bedroom?"

Neelam shook her head, saying nothing.

Mayaram walked towards the bedroom. Neelam followed him.

His eyes scanned the room, then he sat down on the bed with a heavy thump.

"I'm in trouble, Neelam," he said hollowly. "I've come to you for shelter."

"Thank goodness," she said playfully. "Whatever the reason, at least you came."

Mayaram took off his coat, threw it to one side, and began to pull off his shoes.

The bastard! Neelam thought. *Ruined my life, and now he wants even more.*

"Right now, I can't trust anyone but you, Neelam," he mumbled. "That's why I came, even though I knew you wouldn't want to see me again. Neelam, I swear to you, if you give me another chance, I won't give you a reason to complain."

Liar! Traitor! He's come back to use me for some plan of his. But I won't get fooled this time. This time I'll make him pay.

"Don't be angry," he said, reaching out towards her. "I'm telling you the truth, Neelam."

She stayed where she was.

Mayaram stood up and took her in his arms. She said nothing, didn't resist. His dry lips moved over her face. His hands roamed over her body while he whispered empty promises in her ear.

He led her to the bed, and laid her down gently.

Neelam closed her eyes.

He mustn't suspect me... Don't say anything... Don't resist...

She didn't open her eyes until it was all over.

"I'm very tired," Mayaram was saying. "I've been tossed around, travelling between Delhi and Chandigarh all day. I need to rest."

"All right. Go to sleep." Neelam said.

"Here?"

"Why not? It's not like you haven't slept here before."

Mayaram laughed uneasily. He turned over and closed his eyes. Neelam shifted herself away from him and pulled the blanket over them both. Mayaram was asleep almost immediately.

For a long time, Neelam waited. Then she looked at Mayaram intently. He was fast asleep. She said his name softly. No reaction. She called him a little louder. Still nothing. She gently pushed off the blanket and got out of the bed. Noiselessly she walked away.

At the threshold she stopped and looked back.

Mayaram was dead to the world.

She walked to the telephone in the corner of the drawing room. She picked up the directory under the phone and went into the bathroom. Turning on the light, she searched for the number of Aroma Hotel, found it, and memorized it. Then she switched off the light again and came back into the drawing room. Very carefully, terrified that Mayaram might stir, she dialled the number.

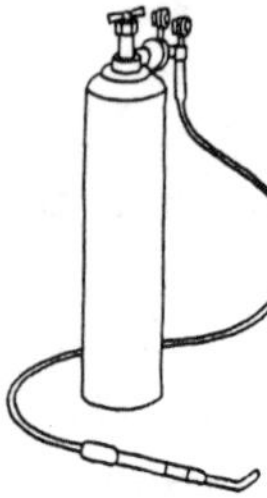

19

VIMAL STOPPED THE CAR in front of New Madras Hotel.

The hotel was a three-storey building, with the restaurant on the ground floor. A uniformed waiter sat outside, smoking a beedi.

Vimal tapped the car horn. The waiter looked up and saw him. Vimal gestured to him to come closer. The waiter threw away his beedi and walked to the car.

"Is Krishnamurti in?" Vimal asked.

"Yes, saheb," the waiter said deferentially.

"Call him. Tell him someone's brought him a message from Mayaram Bawa."

"Very good, saheb." The waiter went in.

In a little while, a huge dark-skinned South Indian came out of the building with the waiter. The waiter pointed out the car to him. Krishnamurti nodded and came to the car. The waiter stayed back.

When he reached the car, Vimal asked, "Krishnamurti?"

"Yes," the man said, looking at him closely.

"I'm a friend of Mayaram Bawa. I have a message from him."

"Tell me."

"Get in. Let's drive a bit and then talk."

Krishnamurti hesitated.

"Oh, get in, swami," Vimal said, opening the door for him. "What are you, a girl? Do you think I'm going to run away with you?"

Krishnamurti got into the car.

Vimal drove ahead. A little distance away, the road was dark and deserted. Vimal stopped the car there. Krishnamurti looked at him questioningly.

"Mayaram has sent you something," Vimal said.

"What?" Krishnamurti said with a trace of eagerness.

"This." Vimal took out the revolver and stuck it into the South Indian's ribs.

Krishnamurti broke out into a sweat. "Enna...enna idhu?" he stammered. "Enna…swami?"

"I'm looking for Mayaram," Vimal said harshly. "I found out you're good friends. I'm sure you know where he is."

"Swami…"

"Talk in Hindustani."

"I don't know where he is."

The revolver moved away from Krishnamurti's ribs for a second, slammed with full force into his nose, and went back to position.

Krishnamurti blubbered in pain. Blood gushed from his nose.

"Tell me Mayaram's address."

"Amritlal might know," Krishnamurti said, wiping off his nose with the back of his hand.

Vimal had heard that name before, from Neelam.

"Who's Amritlal?" he asked.

"He's a waiter at the Regent Restaurant on G.T. Road in Karnal. He usually knows where Mayaram is."

Karnal! Vimal took a deep breath. Amritsar to Jalandhar. Jalandhar to Chandigarh. Chandigarh to Patiala. Patiala to Karnal. And from Karnal, God only knew.

"Get out," Vimal said.

"What?" Krishnamurti said, surprised. He couldn't believe that he was escaping so easily.

"Get out of the car. Forget what just happened. If you try to tell Amritlal or Mayaram about this, I'll come back and slit your throat."

Krishnamurti shuddered, then quickly got out of the car. Vimal drove away.

By the time he reached Karnal, it was eleven o'clock. He had no trouble finding the Regent Restaurant, but he was told that Amritlal hadn't come in that day. He got Amritlal's home address, asked around, and finally reached his house.

Amritlal lay on a settee, oblivious to the world. A young man sat next to him. He introduced himself as Amritlal's neighbour. Vimal asked him what had happened. He said that last night some goons had attacked Amritlal in his home. They'd beaten him brutally and left him half-dead. No one in the neighbourhood had heard anything. Today, a friend of Amritlal's had come from out of town and found him lying on the floor. The friend called a doctor and had had Amritlal patched up. Before leaving, he'd asked the neighbour to take care of him.

Amritlal's entire body was covered with bluish bruises. His skin was gashed in several places, four of his fingers were broken, and a few of his ribs were cracked.

This has to be Harnam Singh Garewal's handiwork, Vimal thought. *Did Garewal get Mayaram's location from this man? Does this man know where Mayaram is?*

"How is he now?" Vimal asked.

"Still very bad." The man said. "Doctor saheb has given him a injection so that he can rest."

"When will he wake up?"

"Tomorrow night. After twenty-four hours."

Even if Amritlal knew something, Vimal couldn't wait that long. It might already be too late! Maybe Garewal had caught up with Mayaram and grabbed the loot…

There was only one remaining lead—Amrik Singh, the inspector from Kapurthala. It would be dangerous to go looking for him, but Vimal had no other choice.

For now, he had to go back to Chandigarh.

He went back the Regent, had something to eat, and then got into the car and set off. But he was tired; he kept nodding off and had to drive slowly. After fifteen or twenty miles, he could no longer concentrate on the road. Somehow he made it to Ambala Cantonment, parked the car at the railway station, rolled up the windows, and fell asleep in the back seat.

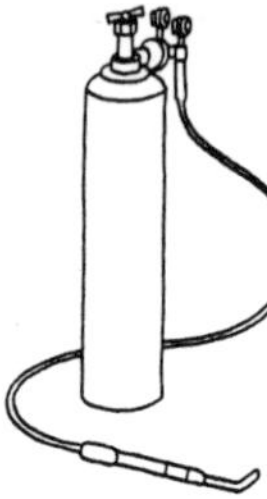

20

IT WAS HALF PAST SEVEN when Vimal stopped the car in front of Aroma Hotel in Chandigarh.

He had slept in the car for about five hours, and felt fresh again.

He walked into the hotel. When he asked the receptionist for the keys to his room, she handed him a message slip as well.

The message had come in at two thirty a.m.: "The thing you're looking for has reached my flat – Neelam."

Vimal's heart beat faster. Had Mayaram really come to Neelam's house?

It had to be. The message couldn't mean anything else, otherwise she would not have called him so late. Neelam had told him that she would alert him immediately if Mayaram turned up.

He tossed the key back onto the counter and turned to go out.

Suddenly his glance fell on the newspaper on a table near the counter, and he stiffened.

Two photographs of his face stared back at him from the front page.

He snatched up the paper.

One of the pictures was an old one, showing him with a turban and beard, probably taken from his Allahabad jail record. The other had been taken after he was arrested in the Delhi bank van robbery, and matched his current appearance closely. Bawa's picture appeared next to his. According to the police statement, the case was solved. Now all that was left was to arrest the criminals, which, according to the police spokesman, would not be difficult now that their pictures had been published. The police expected many people to come forward with information about the wanted men.

The newspaper also had all the details about Vimal's alleged crimes—the same details he'd told the Delhi police after his arrest.

He realized that he was the first person to open this newspaper in the hotel. He quickly folded it up, tucked it under his arm, and glanced at the receptionist. She was paying him no attention, and was looking down at a register. Vimal knew that once the news spread, not only the receptionist, but everyone in the hotel would recall that the person whose photo was in the paper had stayed there.

Lala Haveli Ram's wife in Amritsar was sure to find out the truth as well. She generally slept until noon, but as soon as she woke up and saw the papers, she'd come to know the true identity of her "Channa," her "Makhna," Ramesh Kumar Sharma. And then, all they had to do was to trace Lala Haveli Ram's Ambassador to catch him.

But would the Lala's wife report him? Maybe not. After all, he had served her well. Nonetheless, whether she reported him or not, there was no way he could go back to Amritsar. And whatever he wanted to do here in Chandigarh had to be done quickly.

He walked back to the desk and asked again for the key. The receptionist handed it over without looking at him. Vimal quickly went up to his room, stuffed his clothes into his suitcase, and came back down.

"I'm leaving," he said to receptionist. "Make my bill."

"Yes sir," she said, with a friendly smile.

Vimal paid the bill and walked out of the hotel. He got into the car and drove straight to Neelam's house.

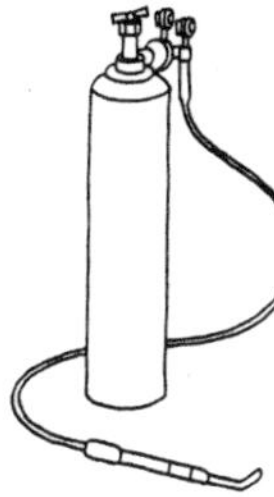

21

"WAKE UP! JAAGO MOHAN PYAARE!" said Vimal, prodding Mayaram with the revolver.

A snore escaped Mayaram's mouth; he twisted sleepily and scrunched up his face. With great difficulty, he opened his eyes. He peered at Vimal. He blinked several times to try to focus. He first recognized the voice, then the face. He sat up as if he'd been stung by a scorpion, and stared at Vimal, wide-eyed, for a few seconds. Finally he said "No!"

Vimal took a few steps back. He saw that Mayaram was wearing only his underwear.

"Get dressed," he said. "And say hello to your old partner. How do you want to do it? Shake hands, or give me a hug?"

"What are you going to do?" he said in a tiny, terrified voice.

"Get up!" Vimal barked.

Mayaram stood up. "That bitch Neelam!" he said, hatred in his voice. "That bitch betrayed me. She was with you from the beginning."

"Shut up!" Vimal growled.

Mayaram swallowed. He began to look for his clothes. Vimal kept the revolver trained on him.

Vimal had reached the flat about ten minutes before. He had found the door open and Neelam gone. Mayaram had been sleeping in the bedroom.

He had searched the entire flat carefully, but there was no trace of the loot from the heist. It wasn't anything small that could be hidden easily, so if it had been in the flat, Vimal would have found it. Which could only mean that Mayaram had stashed it somewhere else.

And where was Neelam?

He watched Mayaram pull on his clothes.

Mayaram recovered his composure while dressing. Now when he spoke, there was no fear in his voice. "You just want the loot, otherwise you'd have finished me by now."

"Obviously," Vimal said. "Mayaram, I warned you right from the start that if you tried to double-cross me, I'd find you, even in hell."

Mayaram licked his lips. "I made a mistake. I underestimated you. Forgive me."

"You'll be punished, not forgiven."

"Are you going to kill me?"

"Why shouldn't I?"

"Without finding out where the loot is?"

"No. First you'll tell me where you've hidden it."

"That means that we could still make a deal."

"No, you'll tell me where you've hidden the loot, Mayaram, without any deal!"

"Not a chance. That's the only trump I hold. Until I know I'm safe, I'm not talking—if I do, you'll make mincemeat of me," he smiled. "I'm hungry. I fell asleep last night without eating anything. I'm going into the kitchen to find something. If you want to find the loot, don't even think of shooting me," he said smugly, turning towards the door.

Vimal let him walk a few steps. Then, once Mayaram was confident nothing would happen, Vimal brought the gun down on his head. Mayaram staggered and fell. Vimal kicked him in the ribs and then stepped back to check his handiwork.

He was happy with what he saw. Things were going well. Time was on his side.

Mayaram pushed himself up slowly. The right side of his face was covered with blood and he looked frightened. His voice quivered as he spoke. "This won't help, my friend! Once I tell you, I know you'll shoot me. You can't force me to talk, Vimal. I guarantee it."

"Really!" A cruel smile played on Vimal's lips.

"Yes."

Vimal switched his revolver to his left hand.

"Stand up!" he commanded.

Mayaram struggled to his feet.

Vimal's right hand closed into a tight fist and connected with Mayaram's jaw with such force that Mayaram crashed to the floor like a felled tree, cracking his skull. Mayaram went still. Vimal dragged his unconscious body onto the bed. Then he pulled out the half-filled bottle and the syringe that he'd taken from Kaul's flat. He looked at the liquid in the bottle. If it had made him talk, it would definitely make Mayaram talk.

But he didn't know how much to inject. Finally, he decided to use everything that was left—he'd probably been given the first half of the bottle himself.

But what if this wasn't the same drug?

"To hell with it," he muttered. "Let's see what happens."

He filled the syringe with the liquid, then pulled Mayaram's sleeve up to his shoulder. He'd never given anyone an injection, but he'd seen other people do it. He jabbed the needle into a likely looking spot on Mayaram's arm, pushed the plunger, and pulled the needle back out of the man's flesh.

He threw away the syringe and looked at Mayaram carefully. His eyes were closed; he seemed oblivious to the world.

"Ustadji!" Vimal said.

Mayaram showed no reaction.

"Mayaram!" Vimal said, close to his ear.

No answer.

Vimal slapped him and shouted his name again. Still no reaction.

He grabbed a fistful of hair and shook Mayaram's head. There wasn't even as much as a twitch.

Vimal grew nervous. He checked Mayaram's pulse and heartbeat, but they were normal.

There was no option but to wait. He moved towards a chair.

Just then, the telephone rang.

Vimal walked to the outer room. He picked up the receiver and held it to his ear, but said nothing.

"Hello!" came Neelam's agitated voice. "Hello! Who is it?"

"It's Vimal," he said. "Where are you?"

"Nearby."

"Why did you leave?"

"I was getting scared. I thought Mayaram might have realized I'd betrayed him."

"Oh."

"Did you find him?"

"Yes."

"What did you do to him?"

"Come see for yourself."

"All right, I'm coming."

Vimal put down the receiver. He went back to the bedroom and looked Mayaram over. He didn't look like he was going to wake up soon. Either the blow had been too hard, or he'd injected too much, or both. Or else it wasn't the drug he'd been given after all. He left the flat and walked up the stairs. There was a jharoka at the landing from which he could see the road. In a few seconds, Neelam walked into view. She was alone.

Vimal sighed with relief. Either she hadn't seen the newspaper, or else she had no intention of telling the police about him and Mayaram.

Neelam entered the flat.

Vimal walked down and went in after her. He closed the door from the inside. Neelam stood transfixed in the bedroom doorway. She turned when she heard him.

"Where were you?" she asked.

"Here," he said offhandedly.

She turned back to look at Mayaram.

"Is he...?" she asked nervously.

"Don't worry," Vimal said. "He isn't dead."

"What did you do to him?"

"Nothing. He's resting. He'll be awake soon."

"I saw today's paper, and the photos of the two of you. I didn't know Mayaram was such a dangerous man. I didn't know you were a criminal, too. Your face is—"

"Whatever my face looks like, that's what I am. I'm no criminal."

"But the paper…"

"What appears to be true isn't always. Neelam, I'm just an ordinary man who's been kicked around by fate too often."

"What do you mean?"

"I'll tell you someday, when there's time. Not now."

She stood there, undecided.

"If you read the newspaper, why didn't you call the police?"

"If it was only Mayaram, I would have," she said hesitantly.

"Why so much concern for me?"

"I don't know." She looked down. "It didn't feel right to report you."

Vimal looked at her intently. Neelam raised her eyes, then shyly dropped them again. In that moment, she seemed to be the purest, most beautiful woman in the world.

"Thank you," Vimal said sincerely. "Thank you."

She said nothing. Suddenly Mayaram stirred.

"Neelam," Vimal said, "go into the kitchen."

"Why?" she asked, bewildered.

"Just go. I need to have a heart-to-heart chat with Mayaram; it's not worth your time."

"Will you kill him?"

Vimal said nothing.

"Vimal, if you kill him, I'll have to believe that you're the person the newspaper says you are."

"All right," Vimal sighed. "I won't kill him. But he isn't worth leaving alive."

"You swear?"

"Will you take a wanted man's word?"

"I will."

"In that case, I swear."

Neelam went out and into the kitchen.

Vimal shook Mayaram violently.

"Ustadji!"

Mayaram stirred.

Vimal pinched his nose and clamped a hand over his mouth. Mayaram began to thrash for air. His eyes fluttered.

Vimal let go.

"Mayaram!" Vimal said. "Mayaram, wake up! Can you hear me, Mayaram? Can you hear my voice?"

Mayaram was silent. Vimal slapped him lightly on his bloodstained cheek.

Mayaram shivered. He opened his eyes, blinked a few times, then closed them again.

"Mayaram, can you hear my voice?"

"Yes," Mayaram said thickly.

"This is Vimal. Do you know who I am?"

"Yes."

"Who am I?"

"Vimal."

"Who else am I?"

"Sardar Surender Singh Sohal."

"And?"

"Girish Mathur."

"And?"

"Banwarilal."

"And?"

"Ramesh Kumar Sharma."

"And who are you?"

"Mayaram. Mayaram Bawa."

"What do most people call you?"

"Ustadji."

"Did you steal all the loot from the heist by yourself?"

Silence.

Vimal shook him again. Then he remembered his own state when he'd been drugged. He remembered that in that state, he could only answer direct questions; he couldn't say anything complicated.

He asked the question another way.

"Do you remember you escaped with all the loot?"

"Yes." The answer came immediately.

"So where's the money?"

"I don't know."

That couldn't be the right answer. Was the effect of the drug wearing off already? Vimal looked closely at Mayaram's face. It was eerily calm, emotionless. It didn't look like he was trying to lie. Then why this answer? Could it be that in the past few days, he'd lost the loot? Had someone else snatched it? Garewal?

"What did you do with it?" he asked.

"I left it at Khanna's house."

"Who's Khanna?"

"My friend."

"Tell me his full name."

"Kailash Kumar Khanna."

"Where does he live?"

"Fourteen, Nizamuddin, Delhi."

"Phone number."

"626816."

"What does Khanna do?"

"He works as a manager in a company."

"You mean he's not a criminal?"

"That's right."

"The loot is at Khanna's house?"

"No."

"Why not?"

"I called him up yesterday. I told him to hide my two suitcases. Not to tell anyone. Not even his wife."

"Do you know where he hid it?"

"No. I haven't called him after that."

"When did he hide the loot?"

"He should have done it yesterday."

"Before you came here, you were with Khanna in Delhi?"

"Yes."

"Why did you leave?"

"Harnam Singh Garewal. He's after me. He wants the loot."

"How did you know?"

"Amritlal told me. Garewal beat up Amritlal and got it out of him."

"You were the one who got Amritlal patched up?"

"Yes."

"What did Amritlal know?"

"..."

Maybe that one was more than he could handle, Vimal thought, and rephrased.

"Did Amritlal tell Khanna's address to Garewal?"

"No."

"Why not?"

"He didn't know it."

"What did he know?"

"Only his phone number."

"Khanna's number?"

"Yes."

It wasn't too hard to find the address that matched a given phone number. That meant that Garewal was ahead of him. He might even have gotten the loot out of Khanna. But there was another thing. Mayaram had gotten a respected member of society involved. If Khanna smelled trouble, nothing would stop him from calling the police. It could be that the police had already recovered the money and Garewal had either escaped or been arrested.

It would be very dangerous to go there. Now that his photos had been printed in the paper, it was risky even to go to Delhi—stepping into Khanna's house would be inviting Death itself.

"Does anyone know about the loot, other than you, me, and Garewal?"

"No one else."

"Why doesn't Khanna know?"

"I only told him to hide the suitcases. I didn't tell him what was inside."

"Could he have opened the suitcases?"

"I don't think so."

"Does Amritlal know about all this?"

"No."

"Did you tell Neelam anything after coming here?"

"No."

Vimal tried to think of who else might know about the loot. "Where did you go after leaving Amritsar?"

"First Delhi…then Karnal…and then here."

"Nowhere else?"

"No."

"Did you meet anyone?"

"No."

"Attar Singh Bajwa in Jalandhar?"

"No."

"Krishnamurti in Patiala?"

"No."

"Inspector Amrik Singh in Kapurthala?"

"No."

"Anyone else?"

"No."

"Are you telling the truth?"

"Yes."

Vimal felt relieved. This meant that the story of the loot hadn't spread much. He wouldn't have to deal with too many people. He walked out into the drawing room, to the telephone. He remembered that you could make trunk calls between Delhi and Chandigarh. He picked up the receiver and dialled the number Mayaram had given him, 626816.

Someone picked up almost immediately.

"Hello," an emotionless voice said.

"Khanna?" Vimal asked.

"Speaking."

"I'm calling with a message from Mayaram. You know who I'm talking about?"

"I know him." There was eagerness in the voice. "Where is he?"

"Mayaram thinks it's best for you if you don't know where he is. But he needs his stuff back."

"What stuff?"

"His two suitcases."

"Oh, right. The suitcases," the voice said guardedly. Somehow, the speaker sounded familiar.

"Mayaram says to bring the suitcases to Chandigarh."

"All right. I'll come. Where are they?"

The person speaking was definitely not Khanna. Khanna knew where the suitcases where—by now, he probably knew what was inside them. In fact, Khanna was the only man in the world who knew where the suitcases were!

Suddenly Vimal remembered where he'd heard the voice before. He put the phone back in its cradle gently.

It was Kaul.

He went back to the bedroom. Mayaram was lying down, eyes closed, face expressionless.

"Mayaram!" he said.

"Yes," Mayaram said, his eyes still shut.

"Can you open your eyes?"

"I don't know."

"Try it."

Mayaram blinked a few times, then looked up blankly.

"Now try to sit up."

With great effort, Mayaram pushed himself up, then dangled his feet to the floor, rested his elbows on his knees, and put his head in his palms. He was swaying like a pendulum and looked as if he might collapse onto the bed any moment. But he didn't.

Now the problem was what to do with him. Vimal didn't know how long the medicine's effects would last. He couldn't leave him here. If Mayaram came to his senses, he might call up the Delhi police and ruin everything. And he couldn't kill him either—he'd promised Neelam.

He made up his mind. He pulled Mayaram to his feet, supporting his weight.

"Walk!" he ordered.

Mayaram began to walk mechanically by his side.

Vimal led him out of the house. He loaded him into the back seat of the car. Mayaram collapsed on the seat like a sack of sand, and closed his eyes again.

Vimal leaned over and searched through Mayaram's pockets. He found a bundle of hundreds inside his coat, and put it into his own pocket.

He went back to the flat. He found Mayaram's suitcase under the bed. He opened it and made a thorough search of its contents. There were ten more bundles of hundreds, which Vimal stuffed into his own pockets. This money was definitely from the heist. There was also a revolver. Vimal took the bullets and put the revolver back. He closed the suitcase and took it out to the car. Then he went into the kitchen.

Neelam was perched nervously on a stool. She stood up when she saw him.

"Neelam," Vimal said amiably, "will you come with me?"

"Where?"

"Delhi."

"Why?"

"To look around."

Neelam hesitated.

"Don't worry," Vimal reassured her, "I'll pay your price—in full."

Neelam looked offended. "I have enough people willing to pay me in Chandigarh. Why should I go to Delhi?"

"Okay, I'm sorry," Vimal said. "Come along as a favour, then. To help me."

"When do we start?"

"Now. I need you to dress up like a bride."

"What?" She looked at him, puzzled.

"You heard me. Pack up whatever you need. I'll be going now, getting bridal clothes for you."

"What about Mayaram?"

"I put him in the car. Don't worry, I'll take care of him."

"You remember your promise?"

"I do."

He came out to the car, started it up, and drove out of the city. Fifteen minutes later, he reached a spot that was deserted, but not too far from a busy road.

Vimal lugged Mayaram out of the car and led him a short distance away. As soon as he let go of him, Mayaram's knees buckled and he collapsed to the ground. Vimal let him fall. He took out his revolver, held it by the barrel, and struck Mayaram three times, with brutally precise blows that snapped three major bones.

Mayaram whimpered once, then fell unconscious.

Vimal reached into his pocket and took out a pen and paper. He wrote on it:

> This man is Mayaram Bawa, the criminal wanted for the heist at the Bharat Bank, Amritsar. He killed two of his partners, Labh Singh and Karamchand, near Khasa, by running them over with his van. Whoever finds him here is requested to take him quickly to a police station (not a hospital).
>
> *Signed,*
> James Bond
> Secret Agent 007
> Licensed to Break the Bones of Double-Crossers

He stuck the paper onto Mayaram's coat with a pin.

He got back into the car, picked up Mayaram's suitcase, and tossed it out the window. Then he drove off. By the time he got back to the city, the shops had begun to open. He stopped the car in front of a shop with a sign saying it sold embroidered clothes for weddings.

Vimal went in. He was the only customer. He watched the shopkeeper's reaction carefully to see if he'd been recognized. To his relief, the shopkeeper gave him a professional, welcoming smile clearly meant for paying customers—not one he'd give a wanted criminal. Vimal bought, without bargaining, an elaborately embroidered red saree with zari work, and red bangles.

There was a jewellers' shop next door. For the bride, he bought an expensive kundan set, a nose ring, two thick golden kadas, and twelve bangles. For himself, he bought a gun-metal ring, a tie pin, and a watch with a golden wristband. Next, he found a readymade garments shop, and bought himself a good suit, a silk tie, and two shirts. At a flower shop, he got the car decorated with flowers. At a paint shop, he bought a can of black paint, a can of white, and a brush. Finally, he went back to Neelam's flat.

He felt satisfied that no one had recognized him, nor had anyone been suspicious of his money.

When he spread out his purchases in front of Neelam, her eyes widened. At first her face lit up like a thousand-watt bulb, but when she looked again at the bridal clothes, she grew serious. Tears glistened in her eyes.

Vimal did not ask her why she was crying. He took the paint and the brush, went out, and changed the number plates on the car.

About an hour later, Vimal sat behind the steering wheel, elegantly dressed in the suit. Next to him, her arm linked with his, Neelam sat blushing, looking as beautiful as a divine apsara, and even more bashful than a real bride.

The car sped towards Delhi.

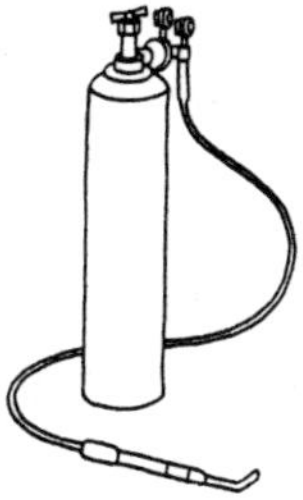

22

VIMAL DROVE BY KHANNA'S BUNGALOW. He saw that a window was open, its curtain drawn back, but he could see no one inside or outside the house.

The newlywed-couple disguise had gotten them through safely. No one had stopped them at the state border, no one had asked any questions, no one had paid any attention. He had dropped Neelam off at a hotel on Alipur Road. There he'd asked a bellboy to remove the flowers from the car, and then he'd driven towards Nizamuddin. He'd instructed Neelam that if he didn't come back by nightfall, she should go back to Chandigarh the next morning.

As he'd left the hotel, Neelam had been as distraught as if she really was his new bride, and he her husband, off to war. There was a heaviness in Vimal's heart as well. As he drove, he couldn't help comparing her to Surjeet. Surjeet had been his wife—yet she was the reason he was on the run, a wanted man. Neelam was nothing to him, but it seemed she cared about him genuinely.

"Wahe Guru sacche Paatshah!" he said to himself. "Strange are the colours in Your world."

Near Khanna's house, Vimal saw children playing on the streets, and there were people sitting on the lawns of the neighbouring houses taking in the winter sun. He couldn't tell what had happened. Had Garewal and Kaul managed to get Khanna to tell them where he'd hidden the suitcases? Had they disappeared with the loot? Or were they still inside?

It all depended on how long Khanna could keep his mouth shut. It had been five or six hours since he'd talked to Kaul. God knows what had happened in the meantime.

There was no way Vimal could keep a watch on Khanna's house from the car. Garewal and Kaul were sure to be alert. They'd be watching for anyone suspicious. Garewal was a dangerous man; he would shoot Vimal without a second thought. The front and back of the bungalow had lawns, and there was open ground on both sides. There was no way to sneak up to the building. It was a strange situation—he couldn't get in, he couldn't go away, and he couldn't wait.

There was only one thing to do.

He had seen a public telephone booth a few buildings away from Khanna's house. He parked the car in front of it and walked into the booth. He dialled Khanna's number. Again, he heard Kaul's voice.

"Hello, Kaul," Vimal said. "This is Vimal. The same Vimal who came to your restaurant in Amritsar to ask about Mayaram. Remember me?"

In reply, there was a sharp intake of breath.

"Give Garewal the phone," he commanded.

"You...you..."

"Stop stuttering. Do as I said. I don't have much time."

Kaul said nothing. The receiver was slammed down on the table. Then there were low, unintelligible voices, like flies buzzing.

He waited.

In a little while, he heard another voice. It was the same voice that had questioned him in Kaul's house.

"Vimal?"

"Yes," Vimal said. "Garewal?"

"Yes. Was it you who called earlier?"

"Yes."

"We were confused earlier, when you called."

"So here I am, to clear up the confusion."

"What do you want?"

"I have Mayaram."

"Very good. Enjoy yourself with him."

"Remember that drug you gave me? I've used the same thing on him."

There was a silence. "Really?"

"What I mean to say is that now I know the whole story."

"So, what do you want?"

"Khanna."

Garewal laughed. "Excellent idea! And how do you intend to get him?"

"Don't you need Mayaram?"

"What do you mean?"

"You don't have the loot yet, and until you get Mayaram, you won't get it."

"You want to deal?"

"Why not? Instead of both of us getting nothing, wouldn't it be better that we get half each?"

"Why would I need Mayaram?"

"Because asking Khanna is getting you nowhere. If you didn't need Mayaram, you'd have found the loot and disappeared. If you're still here, it's because you're waiting for Mayaram."

"Wait. Stay on the line."

"Okay."

Vimal waited, receiver to his ear. He couldn't understand how a demon like Garewal had failed to get Khanna to talk.

Garewal came back on the line. "So what do you want, really?"

"I told you just now," Vimal said. "Half of the loot."

"I heard you. So how do you want to do the deal?"

"First, suggest a place we can both get to."

"I don't want to come outside. I'm safe in here," said Garewal.

"Then how do we meet?"

"Why do we need to meet? Mayaram told you where the loot is. Now you tell me and I'll go get it. I'll leave your half there, and get out."

Vimal laughed incredulously.

"Listen!" Garewal said. "Where are you speaking from?"

"Not far from you," Vimal said.

"I understand. You're at the telephone booth at the corner?"

"Right."

"Why don't you come in?"

Vimal drew a quiet, relieved breath. This was what he'd hoped for, but he'd wanted Garewal to come up with it himself.

"What guarantee do I have that you won't kill me?" asked Vimal.

"What guarantee do you want? You aren't going to believe me anyhow."

"Are you willing to do as I say?"

"What exactly do you want us to do?"

"Have you seen the garage?"

"Yes."

"What's in it?"

"Khanna's car."

"Take out that car and park it on the street somewhere," Vimal said. "Then open the garage shutters and the front gate. But neither your nor Kaul should be in the garage."

"Okay."

"There should be a door connecting the garage to the rest of the house. Is there?"

"Yes."

"What room does it open to?"

"The kitchen."

"Very good. So you put a table and two chairs in the kitchen, and—"

"They're already there."

"Even better. I'll drive my car straight into the garage. You two, sit at the table with the door open, so I can see you from the garage. Your hands should be on the table."

"So that you can start firing at us?" Garewal said jovially.

"I have no such intention," Vimal said. "I'll be empty-handed. Still, if it makes you happy, keep a gun. But put the gun on the table, not in your hands, so that I can be sure you won't start shooting as soon as you see me. All right?"

"All right."

"If I smell the least bit of trouble, I'll be out of there, and you can spend the rest of your life searching for Mayaram."

"But where is he?"

"He's unconscious, in the boot of my car."

"Balle! Anything else?"

"That's it. We'll talk when we meet."

"All right. I'll get the garage cleared out."

"I'm coming."

Vimal hung up.

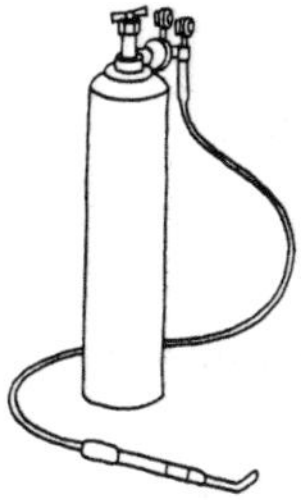

23

THE GARAGE WAS TO THE RIGHT of the building, its shutter all the way up. The main gate to the compound, too, was open, right in front of the garage. Vimal drove in at full speed, not even bothering to hold the steering wheel. His right hand was on the door handle, and his left hand held the revolver.

His eyes darted around as he drove in. The kitchen door would be in the wall to his left.

The car was moving at such speed that he almost had to stand on the brake pedal to get it to stop before it hit the far wall. He registered the kitchen door with a quick glance, and then opened the car door and rolled out swiftly. As he hit the floor, the first bullet from the kitchen door passed four inches above his head and punched through the car.

The car, still in gear, thumped into the back of the garage. The engine continued to growl, and the car pushed against the wall, though not with enough force to do any damage. Just then, the garage shutter began to roll down. Apparently it was an automatic. Garewal must have flipped the switch.

Vimal somersaulted forward, switched the revolver to his right hand, and looked cautiously towards the kitchen. Kaul stood just outside the door, looking shaken. He had a gun in his hand and he was scanning the garage, trying to see Vimal.

Vimal fired from where he lay on the floor.

Kaul's body jerked backwards. The gun fell out of his hand and clattered to the floor. A scream escaped his mouth, and he crumpled to the ground in front of the door.

It had been barely ten seconds since Vimal had arrived.

The shutter of the garage clanged to the ground. Only one bullet had been fired while it was open; Vimal hoped that the neighbours, busy with their work, hadn't heard the shot. Now that the shutter was closed, nothing would be audible from outside.

The car's engine was still running. The fumes from the exhaust pipe were filling up the garage.

A groan issued from Kaul's lips, and he called weakly, "Sardar! Sardar!"

"What happened?" Garewal's heavy voice said.

"I'm hit. A bullet got me."

"Oye, that son of a bitch Vimal!"

Garewal's voice wasn't coming from the kitchen, but from somewhere else in the house. Vimal pushed himself under the car and crawled to the other side. Then he flattened himself against the wall next to the door.

Where he stood, there was a rack filled with tools. He picked up a hammer and moved a little closer to the door so he could see inside. Then, with all his strength, he threw the hammer into the kitchen. All he wanted was to divert Garewal's attention for two seconds. The hammer hit with a loud metallic clang. Something fell down. Right behind the hammer,

Vimal rushed into the kitchen, firing wildly, his head bent down.

A bullet whizzed by Vimal's ear. He hadn't heard the shot—*Garewal's got a silencer,* he thought. He dropped to the floor. Garewal was hiding somewhere behind the other kitchen door. Vimal gripped the revolver with both hands so that the recoil wouldn't spoil his aim.

Garewal leapt across the threshold. Vimal fired.

Garewal yelled and vanished from sight. Something heavy fell with a thump.

Had he been hit?

Vimal sprang up and ran. He had barely come through the doorway when he tripped over Garewal's body and almost fell. He backed away.

Garewal was on his back on the floor, struggling to get up and aim his gun. Vimal gave the gun a hard kick; it spun through the air and landed on the other side of the room.

Garewal growled like an animal and fell back. It sounded like he was having trouble breathing, but Vimal couldn't see any blood.

He listened, but the house was silent. Vimal edged closer to Garewal. His eyes were open; he was staring at Vimal but not moving. He'd definitely taken a bullet, otherwise he'd have leapt at Vimal like a starved wolf.

"Where did it hit?" Vimal asked.

"In the back," Garewal said with great difficulty. "In the spine."

He's done for, Vimal thought to himself. It would be impossible for him to move from where he lay. Vimal walked across the room and picked up Garewal's gun. Then he remembered Kaul. He went back to the garage. Kaul was lying where he'd fallen. He looked at Vimal, terrified. Vimal paid him no attention. He picked up Kaul's gun, too, from where it had fallen, and went back into the house.

Where was Khanna?

He paused near Garewal.

"Where's Khanna?" he asked.

"You're a lucky man," Garewal said, coughing. "My aim was off today for the first time in my life."

"Where is Khanna?"

"I should've killed you in Kaul's flat."

Vimal brought the butt of his gun down on Garewal's forehead. His eyes turned upwards as he blacked out.

Vimal walked through the rooms of the bungalow. He didn't find Khanna, but he did find a woman in the bedroom. Her hands and feet were tied up, and she had a cloth stuffed into her mouth. One eye was swollen shut and there were scratch marks all over her body, some of them crusted with dried blood. She was awake, and stared at Vimal fearfully.

In another room, there were three children. Their hands and legs were also tied up, and their mouths were gagged.

Vimal went back to check on Garewal. He was still unconscious. Then he walked over to Kaul and knelt down next to him. Kaul's eyes focused on him with difficulty.

"Don't touch me," Kaul said.

"Where is Khanna?"

"What did you do to the Sardar?"

Vimal grabbed his nose and twisted it so hard that Kaul's eyes watered.

"Next time, I'll cut it off," Vimal said roughly. "Where is Khanna?"

"He...he's..." Kaul said, gasping, "he's dead."

"How?"

"Garewal went after his wife. Khanna tried to stop him and Garewal started beating him up. I tried to hold him back, but the Sardar goes crazy when he loses his temper. If I'd kept at him, he'd have beaten me up too. He pounded Khanna to death with his bare hands."

Kaul shivered, then he closed his eyes.

"Where's his body?" Vimal demanded. "I didn't see it anywhere."

"Behind the trunks in the storeroom."

"And where's the loot?"

"I don't know. Khanna's wife doesn't know anything. Garewal tried everything he could to get her to talk, but she really doesn't know. All she knows is that Mayaram called, Khanna talked to him, and then he took his two suitcases from the guest room, went out somewhere, and came back empty-handed."

"Doesn't she know where her husband went?"

"No. If she'd known, she'd have told us. It's impossible to hide anything from Garewal."

Vimal took a deep breath.

The only person in the world who knew where the loot from the heist was hidden was dead. Maybe it would stay hidden forever, or maybe Khanna had left the suitcases with friends, who would open them once they heard of his death.

Or maybe they'd give them back to Khanna's widow. She had lost a lot in this whole mess—her husband was dead, and she had suffered untold atrocities at the hands of a demon. If the suitcases made their way back to Khanna's wife—it was a very slim chance, Vimal thought, but not impossible—it ought to be her choice whether to keep the money for herself or to hand it over to the police.

He went back to the bedroom where Khanna's wife was tied up. He took the cloth out of her mouth.

"Behenji," he said politely. "I would like to ask you just one question. I hope you'll answer it correctly."

Being addressed as behenji had a discernable effect on Kiran. It was something a friend would say, not something she would expect from a hoodlum. She looked at Vimal questioningly.

"Do you really not know where your husband left Mayaram's suitcases?"

"I really don't know," Kiran said.

"Okay."

Vimal began to untie her hands and feet.

"Where are those two?" Kiran said in a panicked tone.

"Right here, in your house," Vimal said. "But there's nothing to be frightened about. They're in no state to cause you any more harm."

Kiran looked at him uneasily.

"They can't even get up from where they've fallen." Vimal told her. "The Sardar is in your drawing room. He's got a bullet in his spine and can't move a muscle. The other is on the floor of your garage. He's not going anywhere either."

A savage light shone in Kiran's eyes. She looked at the two guns tucked into Vimal's belt. Vimal followed her gaze, and gave her a little smile.

"Can you give me one of those?" she asked in an icy voice.

"Take both," Vimal said, taking out the guns and putting them on the table, a little out of her reach. He was afraid that as soon as she got a gun in her hand, she'd shoot him. But she'd only just been untied—it would take some time before the blood started circulating. By the time she could move around, he would be far away.

"Can you use them?" he asked.

"Never tried it. Never held one in my hand, either," Kiran said. "But I've seen it in films. Point it at the enemy and pull the trigger."

"And you need to hold it tight, otherwise when you fire, the recoil will make it jump out of your hands."

"So what? I'll pick it up again."

Vimal smiled and walked towards the door.

"Listen!" Kiran called suddenly.

Vimal paused at the threshold.

"Who are you?"

"That's a difficult question. It would take a while to give you a proper answer, and I don't have time. Read the newspaper, you'll find out everything."

"You don't look like a bad man."

"I don't think I am a bad man, but when you read the paper, you'll think I'm the most evil person on earth."

Kiran was silent.

"Okay, then," Vimal said. "Goodbye!"

"Listen!"

"Yes?"

"I am really grateful to you."

"Forget all that."

As he walked out of the room, he saw a light in Kiran's eyes that would make the blood of the most dangerous man alive run cold.

Outside, Garewal was still unconscious.

Vimal reached the kitchen. He found the button that opened the garage shutter and pressed it. When it was two feet above the ground, he removed his finger.

He decided to leave Lala Haveli Ram's car where it was. He went through the kitchen door and walked towards the shutter.

"Hey!"

Vimal stiffened. He turned back to Kaul.

"Are you just going to leave us to the mercy of the police?"

"I've made better arrangements," Vimal said. "I'm leaving you to the mercy of Khanna's wife."

And with a grim smile on his face, Vimal walked out of the garage.

Glossary

Aaho	Yes.
Almirah	A cupboard.
Apsara	In Hindu mythology, one of the beautiful dancing girls of Swarg (heaven).
Badshah, Badshaho	Literally, king; a respectful address.
Balle	A Punjabi exclamation, roughly meaning "wow!" or "wonderful!"
Bauji	Literally, elder brother; respectful address for a man.
Behenji	Literally, sister; respectful address for a woman
Bhagwati Bhavani	A name for the Goddess Durga.
Biba	A term of endearment.
Bibi	Literally, mother; respectful address for an older woman.
Bogie	A compartment in a train.
Bolo Ram	A reference to the chanting done during a funeral ceremony.
Chal oye	Come on!
Chamcha	Literally, spoon; a suck-up or sycophantic follower.
Channa	A term of endearment.
Chappals	Leather or rubber slippers.

Chowkidar	An unarmed security guard or watchman.
Crore	Ten million.
Dacoit	Robber, usually one who attacks in broad daylight, in a group.
Dada	A don or gang leader (street slang).
Darbar Saheb	The Golden Temple in Amritsar; the holiest shrine for Sikhs.
Diwan	A bench without a backrest.
Dupatta	A long cloth draped about the shoulders, worn by women. Usually worn with salwar-kameez.
Emergency	The State of Emergency declared by Prime Minister Indira Gandhi from 1975 to 1977.
Filmi	Film-like, Bollywoodish, often used as a derogatory term for garish costumes.
Godown	Large enclosed storage area.
Granth Saheb *or* Guru Granth Saheb	The Holy Book of the Sikh faith, worshipped at gurudwaras.
Gurudwara	A Sikh temple.
Jaago Mohan Pyaare	"Wake up, Dear Mohan!" (a reference to Lord Krishna); the opening lines of a popular song from a 1956 movie.
Jharoka	A traditional window with a fine stone/steel mesh, usually without windowpanes.

Ji	Used as a suffix to a name to indicate respect, or alone as an address/ salutation, usually by Punjabis.
Jootis	Traditional leather shoes without laces or other fastenings.
Kadas	Thick, ornamental bangles.
Kaki	Literally, aunty; a term of respectful address for an older woman.
Kundan	Uncut stones set in gold, traditionally worn at weddings
Kurta	Long full-sleeved tunic, worn by both men and women.
Lakh	A hundred thousand.
Madrasi	Literally, someone from Madras (now Chennai), but often used erroneously by North Indians for South Indians in general.
Mahi	Dear; a term of endearment.
Makhna	Literally, "smooth as butter"; a term of endearment
Matar-Paneer	A curry made with cottage cheese (paneer) and peas (matar). A popular Punjabi dish.
Oye	Hey!
Pajama	Loose cotton trousers with a drawstring (not nightwear), often worn with a kurta.
Papaji	Literally, father; a term of respectful address for an older man.
Praaji	Alternate pronunciation of Bauji.

Prasad	Small quantity of food given to devotees at a temple, as a symbol of God's blessing.
P. & T.	Post and Telegraph Department
Puttar	Literally, son; address for a younger man.
R.C.C.	Reinforced cement concrete
Roti	Flat wheat bread.
Saheb	Sir.
Salwar-kameez	Women's dress consisting of a loose-fitting pajama (salwar) and a kurta.
Sardar, Sardarni	Titles used to address male and female Sikhs.
Sarovar	A large water tank (pool) in a gurudwara, where devotees take a dip. Here, the reference is to the tank in the Golden Temple.
Sat Sri Akaal	A greeting used at the start or end of conversation. Literally, "God is truth."
Sau rab di	"I swear by God."
Sethani	The wife of a Seth (merchant or businessman).
Shamiana	A large, temporary tent made of brightly coloured canvas and bamboo poles, erected for marriages and parties.
Shera Waliye	Literally, one who rides a tiger; another name for the Goddess Durga.
Sikhe	Used to address a Sikh, usually by other Punjabis.

Tayaji	Literally, uncle (father's elder brother); a respectful address for an older man.
Tehmad	A kind of lungi or sarong worn by men.
Ustad	Teacher, guru; a master of a skill or art.
Wahe Guru	"Wondrous Elightener"; the Sikh term for God
Wahe Guru sacche Paatshah	"God is great"; literally, "God alone is the true King."
Yaara	Friend
Zari	Fine gold or silver thread woven into fabric used in traditional clothing.